MW01281984

STRANDED WITH THE SEAL

STRANDED

WITH THE

SEAL

AMY GAMET

Copyright © 2016 by Amy Gamet
Printed in the United States of America

ALL RIGHTS RESERVED.
No part of this book may be reproduced in any form or by any
electronic or mechanical means, including information storage and
retrieval systems, without written permission from the author, except
for the use of brief quotations in a book review.

CHAPTER 1

A TALL BLONDE woman with a clipboard stepped into the open doorway of the dressing room. "Three minutes, Miss Barrons."

Brooke nodded, holding the cell phone to her ear as she massaged her sore upper arm. "Come on, answer the damn phone."

Hi, I'm busy. Leave me a message!

"Bella, it's me. I need to see you. It's really important," she said, closing her eyes as she exhaled. "I'm…I'm scared. I need you to come out to Colorado. Please. I made you a reservation to fly into Denver Monday afternoon. I sent you an email with the details and…"

The woman with the clipboard was back at the door. "You need to come to the set, now."

"Just a minute."

"Right now, Miss Barrons. We go live in two minutes."

Brooke turned her back to the woman. "I can't go into details now, but it's really important. I'll pick you up at the airport." She hung up the phone and forced the annoyed expression from her face, replacing it with a smile before she turned back around.

"I'm ready."

"Don't forget your veil."

Her stomach pitched violently. "Right." She picked it up from her dressing table and slid the comb into her hair.

It's just a costume. It isn't the real thing.

You're not really marrying a monster.

The woman gestured for her to follow, and they began jogging through clusters of people who all seemed to be standing still.

Brooke's head was throbbing, questions swarming like bees. Maybe none of it was true. Maybe this was a dream and she would wake up engaged to the man she'd thought she was marrying, instead of someone capable of hurting the people she loved.

Her arm ached, the injury to her limb nothing compared to the damage that had been done to her sense of trust. She was in danger. She knew that now, and she had to find a way to escape.

Spotlights came into view, violently bright and focused ahead of her. When the woman stopped in the wings, Brooke continued onto the stage. The band started to play and the title sequence began.

"We've got a great show for you tonight," she yelled over the music. The bee-like buzzing in her head melded with the applause of the crowd, her head spinning. It was too much, every bit of it overwhelming, and she thought her brain might burst with the effort it took to comprehend what had just taken place.

What it meant for her, now that her safety net was gone.

The music stopped and she spun in a circle, the veil flowing around her on the air, gossamer and surreal. She felt nauseated. She would get through this by training and sheer force of will. She would smile and pretend everything was all right—even laugh—then she would run away deep into the night, back to where it all began.

She needed to go there, needed her memories around her now more than ever before, even if it meant going to the edge of hell to get them.

You'll have to get by Gallant.

Sometimes, she didn't know if he was her bodyguard or her babysitter. The man rarely let her out of his sight, and asking him to leave her alone would only rouse his suspicions.

She would do it, distract him with a woman, maybe the one with the clipboard. He would get laid, and she would get the head start she needed to survive.

The music crescendoed as her plans fell into place.

Right on cue, she shouted to the crowd, "Live from New York, it's Saturday Night!"

CHAPTER 2

I T TOOK CONSIDERABLE speed to climb Warsaw Mountain in six inches of unplowed snow, speed that threatened to overcome the traction of Trevor Hawkins' tires at every turn. There'd been another set of tracks in the road, the only sign of humanity in this wilderness, and he imagined they were made by a park ranger or a county truck surveying the road conditions before closing this passageway down for the night.

Your average joe had no business driving on a twisting mountain road in these conditions. Besides the snow on the ground, it was falling at an alarming rate he'd only witnessed once or twice in his life. The lightest wind was enough to create near white-out conditions, and these were not the lightest winds.

He took his foot off the gas just enough to negotiate a sharp turn to the left, the right side of the road bordered only by a guardrail and a hundred-foot drop. That should have deterred him from his mission, but in fact it did the opposite. According to his calculations, that particular turn meant he was just under twelve miles from Steele's mansion, and Hawk would walk through fire if it meant he could get to Steele today.

He thought of his commander, Jax Andersson, and the direct order he'd given Hawk not to pursue this lead. By ignoring Jax, Hawk might lose his position with HERO Force, but if he followed orders, he might lose his mind.

He frowned. He and Jax had damn near started HERO Force together. The Hands-on Engagement and Recognizance Operations team was everything Hawk dreamed of doing with the rest of his life, and losing that would be a hell of a lot worse than just losing a job.

Those were his teammates. His brothers. His family. And when one of them was murdered in cold blood right before his eyes, he knew the day would come when he would find his revenge, even if it meant the end of his time with HERO Force.

Two years he'd been waiting for a chance like this, an opportunity to get Steele. That man had more eyes on him than a housefly, but somehow he always managed to have his hand out of the cookie jar whenever anyone checked.

Through the snow, an image began to appear.

Hawk squinted and eased up on the accelerator, then he saw it clearly. Sixty feet ahead, a red sports car was stopped in the road, a woman in a white coat standing with her back to him.

Hawk pressed hard on the brake, the muscles of his thighs going rigid, and the scene seemed to freeze. The haze of snowfall that had been blinding just moments before was now made of individual crystals.

There was a horrible beauty in the slide of his car across the snow-covered roadway, a slick movement that seemed to slice the world into before and after, and he forced his eyes to stay open when they wanted to close.

He was going to hit her.

It wouldn't be the first time he'd taken a life, but it would be the first time he'd done so accidentally. This woman was innocent, and in that moment he wished ferociously that he could stop his car from moving. He pumped the brake, but his Jeep was little more than a hockey puck sliding across ice, without a nod to his intention.

She turned to face him.

Beautiful.

Her features transformed in fear, her piercing scream reaching him through the glass.

It made it worse that she was pretty, worse that she was young. Worse still that the red car hinted at a spark in her personality. His eyes closed, his will no longer strong enough to keep them open. A guttural cry rose up from his chest just before the impact, the sound of crunching metal and breaking glass overtaking everything.

The force of the accident threw him hard against the airbag, pounding his face like solid wood, but it was her face he imagined, her injuries he worried about as his car crushed the space that had once been between them.

Your hatred brought you here.

If he hadn't been so determined to get Steele, he'd be sitting on a beach right now like the other members of HERO Force. Cowboy would be talking up chicks while Logan read some scientific journal and Jax surfed the waves.

This woman would be alive.

Forcing himself to move his shocked limbs, he pushed against the airbag and stood on shaking legs. He could smell gasoline and his mind shifted into high gear, years of training taking control of his body.

He had to find her. Now.

The Jeep was embedded in the side of the sports car. There was no sign of the woman. He checked beneath the vehicles, then scanned the area, his eyes instantly watering from the biting wind and the swirls of snow.

"Lady?" he yelled. His voice echoed back from tall pine trees, the road he stood on the only seeming break from their dominion. The smell was thicker now, more noxious, and his eyes searched frantically for any sign of her, finally catching on a trail through the snow on the hood of her car.

Racing to the other side, he was dumbfounded to see only virgin snow, untouched. Where the hell was she?

He looked back at the markings on the hood. It was as if she had scampered across the top just before the impact.

Or during it.

He braced himself against the wind and walked into the blinding snow, following the trajectory formed by his Jeep and the path from the hood. "Lady? Where are you?"

A noise sounded behind him, a gentle whoosh like a bed sheet being snapped through the air over a mattress, and for a moment he couldn't place it.

Fire!

"Lady!" he was screaming now, moving faster through the snow. He nearly tripped over her, lying in the snow wearing her white coat. "We have to move," he commanded, stealing a glance at the fire behind him, but even as he spoke he knew she couldn't hear him. He prayed she was unconscious and not dead as he reached beneath her arms and began to pull her up the hill, with only a moment's concern that he shouldn't move her before help arrived.

There was another smell here, the scent of blood, light on the cold winter air. Hawk had smelled enough of it in his life to recognize it easily. He pulled harder, forcing his body to move faster before the inevitable occurred.

Smoke.

Fire.

Gasoline.

As if on cue, the red sports car exploded with a deafening boom, flames and debris shooting outward from the accident, the force of the explosion knocking him backwards into the snow. He stared at a piece of flaming material just ten feet away. They weren't hit, but it was close. Too close, considering his car was bound to be next, and he was packing a lot more fuel for the fire than gasoline.

With a roar he picked up the woman in his arms and began to run. His footsteps fell heavily into the snow, which sucked at his feet and legs, dragging him down. He had to get enough distance between them and the impending second explosion, had to keep this woman safe from further injury.

Already, she might die.

He ran for what seemed a half mile before turning around. He could smell the blaze, but couldn't see it through the snowstorm. A second explosion, bigger than the first, echoed across the mountainside, the shockwave hitting him a moment later. This time,

Hawk kept his footing.

He thought of the weapons he had lost, the car, and how far he was from Steele's house, then he looked down at the woman in his arms. A trail of blood ran down one side of her face, and she was eerily still. He wished for somewhere to lay her down and realized there was nowhere, so he sat in the snow and cradled her in his lap. His big hand reached inside her coat, sliding along her slender neck.

She had a pulse, though it was weak and thready. He reached for his cell phone and found it was not in his pocket. He cursed out loud, knowing it was lost in his vehicle, and he checked the pockets of her coat for one, too, finding nothing. He squeezed her tighter to him.

What had he done? They were alone on a deserted mountain in the middle of a snowstorm, with no cars, no phones, and no shelter.

He worked to shrug off his coat, then laid it in the snow next to them and moved her onto it, knowing what he had to do now. "I'll be back for you as soon as I can, sweetheart."

CHAPTER 3

STANDING UP WAS like unbending metal. Hawk winced as he forced his knees to hold his weight again, realizing he must have sustained an injury in the accident and instantly pushing the thought aside.

It was frigidly cold, and the whipping wind raked his skin like frozen sandpaper. He had about twenty minutes to find or make some kind of shelter and to get that woman the hell into it. He began to jog up the hill, favoring one leg in an awkward hop.

His mind strained to focus on a memory, the map of Warsaw Mountain he'd studied so many times before. But he was eleven miles from his target, and he hadn't paid special attention to the few houses scattered along this remote mountainside. He only knew they existed, and now he prayed they didn't belong to any of Steele's men.

Making his way along the tree line, he looked for any breaks or paths that might indicate a driveway. The road curved to the right in a wide arc and back again, then grew steeper. He thought of the woman and wondered how far he should go before turning around and making his own shelter from the land. He was up to the task, but would she still be alive when he completed it?

Fifty more paces, and he'd go back.

Forty-nine.

Forty-eight.

Forty-seven.

He squinted into the falling snow. There was something up ahead.

A mailbox.

Hawk picked up speed. He ran up the driveway. A cabin appeared, and he was hopeful he'd find someone at home—they'd surely have a vehicle and a way to contact emergency services.

He banged on the door, acutely aware of the passage of time and the freezing temperatures. He banged again and cupped his hands around his eyes, peering through a window.

The cabin was deserted. He turned around in a full circle, taking in the wilderness and seeing nothing that could be of help to him.

He would have to carry her here.

Without missing a beat, he turned back, his mind

no longer in the Colorado mountains. He was back in BUD/S training, in Hell Week, the question of whether or not he could carry on long since forgotten.

Once a SEAL, always a SEAL. As long as his heart was beating, he would go back for the woman.

What had she been doing up here all alone, in weather like this? Either she'd made a bad decision to drive in these conditions, or she'd been as desperate as he to get to her destination.

Minutes ticked by, his breath coming hard. He wasn't used to the altitude and was grateful for his conditioning.

There.

There it was, the biting smell of smoke on the air. He was getting close now, and he sped up faster than he knew he could go. How long had it been since he'd left her side? Fifteen or twenty minutes, maybe more. He could only hope it was soon enough.

The snow was beginning to taper off and he could see her in the distance. She was so still he feared she had died while he was gone. "No," he whispered. "You have to be all right. You have to be."

Reaching the woman, he dropped down beside her and scooped her into his arms, fearing his body would rebel if he gave it any break. Lifting her with him, he stood up with a grunt, and his stare took in the empty road in front of them. The snow had all but stopped, and with the increased visibility he could see all the way to that first sharp turn that had caused the accident.

There was debris from the explosions, random pieces of God knows what, and charred marks on the asphalt where the fire had melted snow, but the cars themselves were gone. Only a blackened trail to a blown-out guardrail remained.

"Holy shit," he whispered under his breath. Both vehicles had been blown over the edge by the second explosion. He looked to the woman. "Maybe I packed a little too much C4."

She was white as a ghost, and he turned, beginning to move once more.

"I don't wanna be no Green Beret," he sang to the rhythm of his footfalls. "They only PT once a day." It was beginning to snow again, fat flakes catching in the wind. "I don't wanna be no airborne ranger." His breath was coming hard, the lining of his lungs burning fiercely from the cold.

He chanted louder. "I wanna live a life of danger." In his head, he could hear his teammates chanting alongside him. "I don't wanna be Marine Recon. I wanna stay till the job is done." Ralph was by his side, the memory of his friend's voice as clear as day to Hawk's ears. "I wanna be a SEAL team member." His teeth began to chatter, but he knew the road to the cabin was not much farther. "I wanna swim the deep blue sea." Icy bits of freezing rain mixed in with the snow, pelting his face. "I wanna live a life of danger. Pick up your swim fins and run with me."

He'd just made it to the driveway when his knee gave out, making him stumble and fall. Somehow he managed to keep ahold of the woman, whose eyes opened slightly.

"Hey," said Hawk quietly. They were clearly confused. They drifted closed again. "There's a house back there," he said. "It's not too far. It's going to be warm, and I'm going to take good care of you." He sensed he needed to talk to her, to keep her with him. The alternative was to let her slip further away, and he knew she was fighting her injuries and the cold for her very life.

"Hey," he said again, lightly shaking her shoulder. "What's your name?"

Her eyes opened the slightest bit and closed without ever focusing on him. "Olivia Grayson."

"Nice to meet you, Olivia. I'm Trevor Hawkins." He gnashed his teeth together as he got up on one knee. "Some people call me Hawk."

He could just see the cabin up ahead, though the light of day was beginning to wane. He had to make it there, had to get both of them there to keep them alive. He forced his leg to bear weight, clenching his teeth on a groan and pushing himself forward.

He carried her, the muscles of his arms on fire. A punishing gust of wind nearly blew him over, forcing him to stop walking and brace himself against it. His energy was nearly depleted, his determination battered. He snarled at the sky. "Do what you want to me," he cried out, "but none of this is her fault. You take care of her, no matter how much you hate me."

The wind slowed and he trudged the remaining distance to the door.

He had to put her down, needed to find a way inside or to break a window. Only when he rested her on the snow did he realize he'd left his jacket back at the accident scene. Looking around, he found a metal watering can to the side of the door and used it to smash one of the sidelights beside it. He reached in and unlocked the door, exhaling a quivering breath, then opened it.

He dragged her inside.

Every part of his body was begging for relief, but he had to see what her injuries were, had to get her warm, had to see if anything could be done to help her. Bending down once more, he picked her up and carried her to a couch, putting her down gently until his knee gave way in protest.

He kicked off his wet shoes and pulled off his socks, desperate to get out of the cold pieces, and knew she must be far colder than he. First things first. He had to call an ambulance. "I'm going to find the phone." Turning around, he got his first good look at the cabin.

The room was dominated by a large stone fireplace. Snowshoes hung on the wall, along with a winter scene that made Warsaw Mountain look far better than Hawk's current experience with it. He wandered into a small kitchen, an old-fashioned wall phone hanging there. It had no dial tone, and he swore mightily.

Turning down a dark hallway, he found the thermostat set to forty-five and bumped it up to seventy, then checked the bedrooms for a phone before grabbing two blankets and a pillow and returning to Olivia.

Her pants were wet on her thighs, ice crystals forming in places. "Let's get you out of these clothes." He started with her shoes—leather boots meant more for fashion than for snow—then he took off her socks and peeled her wet leggings down and off.

Her skin was blue and he cringed, covering her legs with the blanket.

You did this to her.

"You need to get warm," he said. He took off her coat and was surprised when he saw her shirt said "Bride" in sparkling gold letters. She barely looked old enough for marriage.

He'd seen shirts like that on women in bars, celebrating their bachelorette parties. He carefully slipped it up and over her head, noting the fresh bruises on the left side of her body where she must have landed. The dark peaks of her nipples were visible in his peripheral vision, but he kept his eyes trained on his hands as he pulled the blanket up to cover her. "I'll go see if I can find you some clothes."

Hawk rubbed his hand over his mouth as he made his way down the quickly darkening corridor. If she was wearing a bra, it was damn near see-through. Or she wasn't wearing one at all. His body twitched to life and he chastised himself for the thought. She was hurt, nearly frozen to death, and she needed his help. Only a pervert would get hard from that.

Or a red-blooded man who hasn't gotten laid in too long.

He shook his head, forcing his thoughts back in line.

The larger of two bedrooms had two dressers, one with a woman's wardrobe, one with a man's. He threw the wet clothes into a corner and pulled out a pair of pink long johns for her to wear before shucking off his own wet clothing with a sigh. His arms were heavy as he pulled on a pair of sweat pants and a hoodie.

He returned to the living room and sat gently on the edge of the couch. He began to examine her head injury.

She recoiled. "Ouch."

He looked at her face, her eyes still closed, and a wave of protectiveness swept through him. "Can you hear me, sweetie?"

"Mmm hmm."

She was responding to him. That was good. "How

are you feeling?"

"Cold."

"Is that it?"

"My head hurts."

"I know. I need to look at that, okay?"

"And my fingers hurt."

He pulled her hands out from under the covers, finding a diamond engagement ring on her left ring finger. The hand was swelling, and he fingered a dark bruise on her wrist, his brows coming together in concern. Gently, he placed her hand in his, and a tingle ran up his arm when his palm brushed hers.

"Squeeze my hand as hard as you can," he said.

She grabbed on to him, her grip surprisingly strong.

"Good." He turned her wrist backwards, his eye catching another bruise, this one high on her arm and the size and color of a purple grape. The hair on the back of his neck went up and he frowned, lifting her arm and looking for the bruise's telltale companions.

"What's wrong?" she asked.

"I don't think your wrist is broken," he evaded.

There. Three matching grape bruises on the other side of her arm. The accident hadn't caused them. Someone hurt her before he did, and the knowledge curdled in his stomach as his eyes went back to the rock on her wedding finger. Odds were good the man who'd given it to her was the same one who dug his fingers into the tender flesh of her arm.

It took some doing, but he managed to get the ring off and tucked it inside his pants pocket before focusing his attention on her head.

This time she didn't pull away as he examined her. "It looks pretty superficial," he said, but that didn't mean she didn't have a concussion or worse where he couldn't see.

"Are you a doctor?" she asked.

"No. Do you remember what happened?"

She made a little sound like a child crying. "I'm so cold."

"I have warm clothes for you."

Her eyes opened at that, and she moved to sit up, the blanket beginning to fall before she covered herself. "Where are my clothes?" she asked.

"I took them off. They were wet. It's okay." He helped her put on the long johns, not wanting her to feel more vulnerable than she already did. He had two sisters and would just as soon knock any guy silly who took advantage of a woman. Sitting by her feet, he pulled back the covers and helped her put on the matching pants.

"Thank you," she whispered, averting her eyes. "Do you have any aspirin?"

She thought this was his house. He cocked his eyebrows, unsure if he should correct her and deciding it was easier to let it go. He found some painkillers in the bathroom and turned the water on, but nothing happened.

He cursed under his breath. The pipes were probably frozen.

She was sound asleep when he returned. He popped the painkillers in his own mouth and swallowed them dry.

He found firewood on a covered porch out back and quickly made a fire, then took a candle from the mantel and went to check out the water pipes in the basement. They were wrapped with wires he recognized as heat tape, and plugged into electrical outlets in the ceiling.

He located the electric meter and fingered the wire tag that held the outer ring in place to guard against tampering. He found a pair of wire cutters on a small workbench and cut through the wire. The metal ring around the glass meter needed a little encouragement from a screwdriver, but then it came off, allowing Trevor to remove the entire glass meter from its backing.

Two plastic tabs covered large prongs, and he removed them before plugging the meter back in and replacing the metal ring. The wheel on the meter began to spin, showing electricity was running through it.

Somebody would be facing a large fine from the electric company for breaking the wire seal, but defrosting the pipes was far more important at the moment, and if there was an electric pump on the well, they also needed the electricity to bring water into the house at all.

Back upstairs, Trevor patched the hole in the window with cardboard from a cereal box, then wrapped the second blanket around his shoulders and sat down on the couch opposite Olivia to check his knee. It was badly swollen, with a red and purple contusion from the top of his kneecap to the top of his shin. He put pressure on the kneecap and hissed as he inhaled.

This was not how this day was supposed to have gone. His only consolation was that she seemed to be okay and the snowstorm that had caused their accident would likely prevent Steele from leaving Warsaw Mountain this evening as the intel claimed. According to the weather report Hawk heard before he left Denver, it was supposed to be even worse to the east, which was where Steele needed to drop off the shipment.

Come morning, the woman would be feeling better and he could find another way to get in and out of Steele's compound. Without any weapons or ammunition, a vehicle, and without any C4. "I knew I was going to run out of C4," he muttered, pulling the blanket up to his chin.

When daylight came, he'd make a new plan. But no matter what happened, he wasn't leaving this mountain until Steele was dead. He owed it to Ralph.

His eyes drifted shut. He was asleep within minutes.

CHAPTER 4

LOGAN O'MALLEY WAS reading in his childhood bed, his feet dangling off the end like the lanky giant he was. His plan to go to the beach with the rest of HERO Force had petered out before it really got off the ground, with Cowboy and Matteo being the only ones to actually make it to Cabo San Lucas. Seemed those two clowns were the only ones who actually did a lot of things.

Logan certainly hadn't planned on spending the week in his hometown, meaning only to stop off for a night or two before heading to Cabo, but his mother was so happy to have both her children home at the same time, he'd decided to stay.

The door opened and his sister walked in without knocking. "Jesus, Logan. Put some fucking clothes on."

He looked down at his striped bikini briefs, half-covered by a Batman comforter. "It's my room, Charlotte. And when did you start talking like that?"

"Janie and Sarah are coming over to get ready for the reunion, and you have the better bathroom. And I've been talking like that for most of my adult life, thank you very much. Now I'd like you to pack up and go shake your money-maker someplace else."

He frowned. That wasn't true. She'd only been talking that way since marrying Loser Rick fresh out of high school, and she never lost the colorful vocabulary after she divorced him. But the rest of her little speech piqued his interest. Out of all of his sister's friends, they were getting a visit from his personal favorite, and he smiled a wolf's grin. "Sarah Davenport?" She'd been a cute little prude in high school, all buttoned-up sweaters and perky little tits.

Charlotte pointed a manicured red nail at him. "Don't even think about it. The last time you were home, Trisha Palmieri wouldn't speak to me for a month afterwards. You said you'd call her."

"I did call. I left my wallet on her dresser and I had to get it back." He winked. "Besides, you don't even like Trisha Palmieri."

"That's not the point. Just because you went from a geeky geek to a hot geek doesn't mean you can go all Don Juan on my whole high school yearbook."

"We're not in high school anymore, Sis. I can date your friends if I want to."

Logan's cell phone chimed, and she turned to face him, hand on her hip and a gleam in her eye. "Then I can date yours, too."

"Sure."

She smiled widely and he instantly realized his mistake.

"Except Cowboy," he said, reaching for his phone.

Charlotte scowled. "One of these days, you're not going to have any say in the matter. He likes me, too, you know."

Logan screwed his face up and blew out air, but he knew she was right. He'd seen the way his HERO Force co-worker looked at his sister, and he knew exactly what the bastard was thinking when he did it. Hell, it was written all over his face that he wanted to get into Charlotte's pants, and he probably would have done so already if he and Logan didn't work together.

Cowboy was a great guy to have on the Teams, and even better with HERO Force, but he was about as far from a stand-up guy where women were concerned as a guy could get, bedding every pretty girl within a fifteen-mile radius, and taking in more area than that for the hot ones. He imagined Charlotte on Cowboy's arm, and squeezed his eyes shut.

"I don't want to hear this." He answered his phone. "Logan."

"It's Jax. I need you to do something for me."

Logan's pulse picked up speed. Jax hadn't given

him any reason to think he was pleased with Logan's performance since hiring him for HERO Force six months ago. Sometimes Logan was all but sure Jax regretted it.

Charlotte crossed her arms and whispered, "I'm not a virgin, brother-boy, and you don't get to decide who I fuck."

Logan frowned and gestured for her to be quiet. "Shoot," he said into the phone.

Jax's voice was like a bark. "I need you to trace Hawk's phone."

Logan's stomach sank and tightened into a knot.

It doesn't mean Hawk did anything wrong.

"Something wrong?" Logan asked.

Charlotte cocked her head and he waved her away, even as blood rushed to his cheeks, turning them hot. He moved to his computer. She didn't leave.

"I just need to find him," said Jax.

"He's not answering?"

"Just trace the damn phone, Doc."

Logan pursed his lips as the program loaded. Doc was the nickname the other guys gave him when he joined HERO Force because he was a medical doctor and a Ph.D., but the nickname hadn't really stuck and sounded especially forced on Jax's lips. Logan swallowed hard against his throat, which had gone suddenly dry.

You knew you shouldn't have told Hawk anything.

Logan's fingers moved stiffly over the keys, typing in a series of codes and password overrides. "I'm almost there."

You'll type in his GPS and it will come up with Cabo or Miami or something like that.

He cut and pasted the serial number for Hawk's phone into the tracking software, convinced the screen would say anyplace in the world except the one place Hawk shouldn't be. The screen refreshed, a series of coordinates and a general location searing into Logan's retinas.

Damn it all to hell.

His balls would be on the chopping block for this, his coveted and beloved position with HERO Force nothing more than a memory. This was the only thing he wanted to do, the only team he wanted to do it with. He licked his lips and found his voice. "Warsaw, Colorado."

Jax exploded into a string of swearing that put Charlotte's vocabulary to shame. "Hawk's gone rogue, and now we have to stop him before he does something stupid."

Logan pinched the bridge of his nose. "This would probably be a good time to tell you he's been asking for the latest intel on Steele."

"*What?*"

Charlotte raised her eyebrows and sucked in a breath, the look she gave him clearly saying, *You're in trouble.* Logan gestured violently toward the door, but she ignored him and turned on the TV.

Jax was screaming in Logan's ear. "Why the hell didn't you tell me?"

"I assumed you knew."

"How much did you give him?" asked Jax.

"Daily updates this week. When I heard the phone, I assumed it was him because he didn't call yet today."

Jax exploded again and Logan let the insults wash over him. "I'm sorry, sir," he said, reverting to his more formal address for his boss. "I should have checked with you first."

"Damn straight you should have checked with me! Give me his coordinates."

Logan clicked to another screen and rattled off a series of numbers. "Sir, I'm only a few hours from there. I can drive up and check on him myself."

Charlotte hit him on the back and he gaped at her. *What was that for?*

She shook her hand at the TV, where traffic was crawling through snow-covered streets. The headline at the bottom of the page read, "Storm of the Century Strikes Colorado Mountains."

Logan reached for the remote control and turned up the volume. "Scratch that, Jax. We have a problem. As we speak, Warsaw Mountain's in the middle of the worst blizzard they've had in years." The scene changed to a round and balding weatherman in front of a color-coded map. "Hang on," Logan said into the phone. "The weather's coming on."

"...a northeasterly direction. Conditions rapidly deteriorated through the early morning hours, resulting in the governor declaring a state of emergency for the northern part of the state here in red, as well as the closure of all interstates and local expressways, with a ban on unnecessary travel in place for Dublin and Marcos Counties. With more than three feet forecasted for the highest elevations, we don't anticipate that travel ban to be lifted anytime soon."

Logan rubbed his lower lip. He knew as well as anyone what would happen if they couldn't get to Hawk before Hawk made it to Steele. *Total annihilation.* Sweat broke out on Logan's palms and brow. "They're expecting three more feet on Warsaw Mountain," he said into the phone.

"Did Hawk make it to Steele?" barked Jax. "Is he at the top of the mountain?"

"Checking the coordinates now." Logan copied and pasted the numbers into a map program, the view zooming in from the globe to the United States to Colorado in a whoosh. A pinpoint appeared. "Not yet, sir. He's eleven miles from the compound."

Another stream of profanity raged in Logan's ear, followed by a heavy, angry huff. "Then we're fucked," finished Jax. "Two goddamn years and he's going to go in there and blow everything to hell, and HERO Force to hell with it. All for Ralph, like he thought I wouldn't take care of it."

Logan held his breath. His eyes met Charlotte's as she mimed her concern. But he knew better than to speak, the temptation to fill the silence nothing compared to his desire to slip unnoticed from this conversation. He didn't know who Ralph was, but the one time he'd heard the name—while Jax and Hawk were screaming at each other across the conference table about Steele—told him the topic was more explosive than nitro.

The voice of a newscaster trailed on in the background. "...some concern about the structure, as it is scheduled to be torn down and rebuilt in the spring after failing an engineering inspection in the fall."

Jax's voice was deep and foreboding. "Where is he now?"

Logan refreshed the software, wondering if this was how the next hour would be spent—tracking Hawk's phone as they watched him approach the Steele mansion, stay for a while, and retreat. The screen repopulated and Logan frowned. "He's not moving."

"What do you mean?"

"His coordinates are exactly the same, right down to the seconds. He hasn't moved at all since our last scan."

Jax growled. "Wait two minutes and try it again."

A knock at the door and it opened, the alabaster

face of Sarah Davenport contrasting sharply with her coral-painted lips. Her eyes dropped to Logan's nearly naked body, roving up his legs and pausing too long where his brief-clad body bent in the chair before making her way to his face. She smiled tentatively, and Logan imagined those coral lips giving way beneath his kisses before Charlotte corralled her into the hallway and shut the door behind them.

God, it would be good to get laid, and from the look on Sarah's face, that was a distinct possibility. He shook his head as he stood and pulled on pants, then sat and refreshed the screen again. "Same coordinates."

"What does it mean?"

"Could mean he left his phone there. Could mean he's taking a leak, or a nap. Whatever the reason, he isn't moving."

"He might be stuck in the storm," said Jax.

Logan bobbed his head. "Possible."

"If he's stuck in the storm, he hasn't killed anyone yet."

"True." Logan knew what was coming.

"How fast can you get yourself to Gamma Squadron headquarters?"

"Couple hours."

"Then do it."

The line went dead in his hand.

So much for Sarah Davenport.

He only mourned the promises of those coral lips for a moment, because he knew his HERO Force brothers were more important than any woman could ever be.

CHAPTER 5

S HE SMELLED LIKE honey and musk, the scent surrounding him as he moved closer to her sleeping form. It was so cold, and he craved her warmth as much as he craved the curves of her body cushioning the hard planes of his own.

There was an ache deep in his hip like he'd worked out too hard, another in his quads. What the hell had he been doing? The woman was beginning to fade, her scent more ethereal, and he lunged for her, inhaling the smell deep into his lungs. The tiniest touch of woodsmoke lingered on her skin, and he opened his eyes, confused.

Where the hell was he?

So damn cold. Even with a thick comforter, he was chilled clear through to his bones. He worked to remember where he was.

He could hear the crash of the accident, remember running on his aching knee, the unconscious woman in his arms. The cabin.

He looked around, taking in the dark room and the fire that had nearly burned out. Pursing his lips, he exhaled, half expecting to be able to see his own breath, but could not.

He took in the sleeping form on the couch opposite him, immediately recognizing the woman from his dream. *Olivia.* He needed to be beside her, needed to feel her warmth against his skin, just as he had dreamed. He sat up, pulling his covers with him. Crossing to her, he placed his hands on her cheeks, then her forehead. For the second time that day, he wondered if she'd died from her injuries.

Fear trickled down his spine like drops of icy water. He kneeled beside her and felt her neck for a pulse, finding a steady beat.

Alive, then—but surely not well. A hard shiver shook his shoulders. What had happened to the furnace? The first thing he did was to turn the heat up, but clearly it wasn't working. He'd check it out in the morning. Right now, he needed more wood for the fire, and he stood, resolute. Intense cold always reminded him of BUD/S training, and being repeatedly showered with a fire hose in the freezing cold.

It reminded him he could withstand anything.

It was what he was trained to do.

As he stepped onto the porch, the wind pushed him full in the face. Bracing himself, he filled his arms with firewood, then went inside and skillfully laid the logs on the embers. He covered Olivia with his comforter and slipped in behind her. It was a tight squeeze on the narrow couch, but they needed each other's warmth more than he needed to be comfortable.

He pulled her tightly against his body and wrapped his arms around her. She was cold enough that she seemed to suck out the little warmth he had left in his own body, like he was lying in bed with a popsicle. He rubbed her arms and slipped her leg between his own, willing the heat from his body into hers.

"You're going to be okay," he whispered into her ear, wondering if she could hear him and fearing she could not.

This was his fault. He'd done this to her.

Guilt was like an aching pit he was being pulled into, the knowledge of his own responsibility for her current state overwhelming him. What if she never woke up again? What if she couldn't walk, or needed medical care he couldn't get her here?

He rubbed his cheek on her back. "I'm sorry."

The fire began to crackle and catch. He took in her profile, the golden light of the fire illuminating her skin. There was a dark bruise beneath her eye and another on her forehead, but neither could hide what a beautiful woman she was, with fine bone structure and lushly rounded lips.

Up close her features shone with a natural kind of beauty that stirred something deep in his belly. He ran his hand up to her shoulder and down to her waist, feeling the womanly rise and fall of her silhouette.

He gritted his teeth together. He had to get her warm, but getting turned on was not part of the bargain. He forced himself to look at the fresh bruises that marred her honeyed complexion.

She was his responsibility.

"I won't let you down," he whispered. She half turned at the sound of his voice, clearly startled.

"Olivia?"

Her teeth started chattering and her torso began to shake.

"Come here," he said, shifting so she could roll her chest toward him. "I'll keep you warm."

She did as she was told, but as soon as she started to move she called out in pain.

"What's wrong?"

Her only answer was to press her head hard against his chest and cry. He gently threaded his fingers through her hair and she swatted them away.

"Does your head hurt?" he asked.

"Mmm hmm."

He wished he could make the pain go away, wished he could take back the accident entirely. Why had fate put her in his path? He shook his head. He was so close to finally getting revenge.

His brow creased, honor and revenge colliding in his mind. He needed to take care of Olivia, and he needed to take Steele out, once and for all.

Most of all, what he needed was a plan to do both, without sacrificing one for the other.

CHAPTER 6

COWBOY GRABBED A fistful of cheese puffs and belched, his eyes never leaving the television. "Brooke Barrons is fucking hot."

Matteo shrugged one heavily muscled shoulder and opened another beer. "In a totally stereotypical American beauty kind of way, I suppose."

"We ain't in the military no more, Red, so I can ask. Are you gay?"

"No."

We've got a terrific show for you guys tonight…

Cowboy gestured to the TV. "So give me a *booyah* when I say Brooke Barrons is fucking hot, not some bullshit answer about the sociological implications of stereotypical beauty."

"You almost sounded intelligent just now."

"I mean, shit, look at her. That hair. Those tits.

That tiny little waist, and legs so long they could wrap around you and squeeze the living daylights out of your ass."

"From her outfit, I'm thinking she's off the market."

Cowboy sneered at her formfitting T-shirt with "Bride" written on it and the long veil flowing from her head. "Probably marrying some Hollywood metrosexual like all those movie stars do. I swear, some of them actresses can throw their husbands across the room, unless a high wind beats 'em to it."

A loud crack of thunder made the hotel walls shake.

"Fucking Cabo San Lucas," the men said in unison.

Live from New York, it's Saturday Night!

Matteo took a long swig of beer. "What do you think the others are doing?"

"Let's see…Jax is getting fitted with a shiny new stick up his ass, Logan is white-boy dancing at a bar with his mother, and Hawk is sitting in a dark room, brooding."

"Pass me the cheese balls."

Cowboy pointed into the bowl. "These here are what real men call cheese puffs. They ain't no cheese balls."

"Whatever. Pass 'em over here." Matteo took a handful. "You're not far off about Hawk. What's the matter with him lately?"

Cowboy moved for another beer. He was going to feel like bloated roadkill in the morning. He considered what to tell Matteo. "Ain't just lately. Been since Ralph died."

"What happened?"

Cowboy eyed the second newest member of HERO Force, sizing him up. Matteo was a former SEAL—everyone but Logan was a SEAL—but Matteo was the only one who came from a different team. It was Jax who wanted Matteo on HERO Force, and Cowboy had yet to figure out why.

Matteo was a sniper, and a hell of a good one, but snipers were nothing special in the military. No, there was another reason Jax wanted him on the FORCE, and Cowboy was determined to figure out why.

"Tell you what, Red, you tell me what puts the sparkle in your flapjacks, and I'll tell you what you want to know about Hawk."

Matteo rolled his eyes. "Not this shit again."

Cowboy turned to the window, a lighted palm tree whipping fiercely in the wind. He was getting to Matteo. He could feel it. One of these days he'd tell Cowboy everything he wanted to know. "Got to be something."

"I was the best sniper in my class."

Cowboy curled his lips and shook his head. "Has to be more than that."

"And I'm a pilot. A good one."

"Keep going."

Matteo shrugged. "You'll have to ask Jax. Maybe he likes my full, round ass."

Matteo was holding out on him, but Cowboy couldn't help but smile. The leader of HERO Force was notoriously attracted to women with large rear ends. "He is an ass man."

Thunder rolled in the distance.

"Fucking Cabo San Lucas," they chimed.

Cowboy stood up and the world banked left. Fuck it. He'd get the goods on Matteo sooner or later. "All right, you want to know what happened, I'll tell you. We were doing surveillance on a guy named Steele, some badass billionaire with an import/export business. Trouble is, he imports and exports shit like drugs and human beings, with the occasional shipment of firearms."

"Why hasn't he been caught?"

"Because he's got tens of thousands of shipments coming in and out of the country every year, and only a handful are illegal. He's got hundreds of employees and an inner circle that covers his back. The feds haven't been able to pin him with anything." He reached for the cheese puffs, but pushed them away, then ran his hand over his forehead. "Ralph was getting close, really close. He and Hawk infiltrated Steele's compound, Ralph in the lead, Hawk on his six.

Only Hawk walked out of there that night."

"He blames himself," said Matteo.

"Steele's men held him down while he watched Ralph die a slow and painful death. That's not the kind of thing you just put out of your mind."

Matteo made the sign of the cross, mumbling something under his breath.

Cowboy drained his beer. There wasn't enough alcohol in the world for this story. Never had been. If it were up to Cowboy, getting Ralph's killer would be HERO Force mission number one, but Jax would never allow it.

He sniffed and shrugged his shoulders. "Of course, by the time the cops got there the body was gone. No evidence of any wrongdoing, that sort of thing. That's what happens when you've got an army of minions just waiting to cover your tracks."

"They find him?"

Cowboy was starting to get drunk. Real drunk, the kind that made you wish things were different at the same time you stopped caring at all. "No. And he's got a wife and little kid who was born after he died."

"No wonder Hawk's obsessed."

Another crack of thunder seemed to shake the world, and it crossed Cowboy's mind that God didn't like this story any more than he did.

"Fucking Cabo San Lucas," they chimed.

CHAPTER 7

OLIVIA WAS AWARE of the headache long before she opened her eyes, the pain pulsing and seeming to fill her entire experience. When she shifted her position, a wave of nausea bubbled through her stomach and she squinted her eyes open a tiny crack.

That made it worse.

She closed them again.

I think I'm going to be sick.

She curled in on herself, wrapping her arms around her middle. She wanted this pain to go away, wanted the edges of her consciousness to be less sharp and aching. She licked her lips. Her mouth was so dry. She needed to find some painkillers and a glass of water, but she'd have to get up, and that was far more than she felt capable of doing.

An arm reached across her midsection and she

gasped. It curled up her chest, the hand grazing her breast.

She held her breath.

Who the hell is that?

Terror sluiced through her. She snuck another peek at the room around her, her eyes focused on the embers glowing brightly in the fireplace, then shifted to take in a gold-flecked bottle on the mantel. Alcohol. The man moaned and snuggled closer to her back, and she squeezed her eyes shut.

She must have been drinking.

Light-headed with panic, she worked to keep her breathing as normal as possible. She took stock of her body, clenching her thighs and the muscles inside her pelvis. Neither were sore or tender like they would be after sex, which didn't help to explain the man currently pressed against her backside, or what felt like his growing erection.

She inched away, pain shooting through her left shoulder and down her side and surprising her into stillness. She struggled to remember what she'd been doing before she went to bed, a memory like the smallest thread she could pull and trace back to a sweater, but was unable to think beyond her sore body and the throbbing inside her skull.

She couldn't remember anything.

What if he slipped something in my drink and brought me here without me knowing?

Her senses were instantly on high alert. As slowly as she could, she eased away from the man and rolled from the couch onto the floor, the movement once again throwing pain through half her body and making her previous headache seem like child's play.

She looked back at the still-sleeping stranger, menacing with his sharp jaw and dark stubble. Her eyes stuck on the wide set of his enormous shoulders. There was strength there, enough to make her willowy limbs quake with the possibilities of what had happened to her.

Come on, Olivia. Think! How did you get here?

The man rolled to his side, his silhouette dramatizing his bone structure and physique. He was so masculine, like an image of primitive man in a museum somewhere, the kind of man she would have found attractive if her reaction were not threaded with this heavy fear.

The kind of man she'd have a hard time escaping from in her current condition.

She needed to get the hell out of here before this guy woke up.

As she carefully crawled away with her good arm, the pounding in her head begged her to be still as her panic egged her on. There'd be time later to coddle her headache, once she was safe and sound and out of this place. She needed to get home.

The thought resonated in her head like a punchline

and she froze, her eyes widening.

Home—a word that should conjure feelings of security and peace—brought up only a blank page in her mind. She mentally shook herself.

Come on. *Home.*

Nothing.

Her breath came faster, too fast now.

The man mumbled something under his breath and shifted in his sleep, forcing her to move. If she couldn't even remember where she lived, there was no more doubt in her mind that the sleeping creep had drugged her before bringing her here last night.

Dear God, she hoped it was last night. She swallowed the possibility she'd been here longer.

As quietly as she could, she used the coffee table to lift herself to a stand. An overwhelming wave of dizziness had her knees buckling, and she fell back down to the floor, her knee banging the coffee table with enough force that her eyes immediately shot to the man.

His eyes opened. He stared at the ceiling.

He was going to grab her and have his way with her, and suddenly she wished for the vacancy in her mind to rescue her from this reality again. She wanted to throw up. Damn it, she was going to throw up. She hugged her knees, fighting the need to vomit.

"Are you okay?" the man asked.

Now she'd done it, woken the bear who was bound

to try to keep her in this cave. His voice was deeper than she'd been expecting, its tone vibrating in her chest. She looked to a doorway, knowing it was too far for her to run.

She had to pretend she wasn't afraid, had to keep him at ease. She threw him what she hoped looked like an embarrassed glance over her shoulder. "I feel sick to my stomach."

"Does your head hurt?"

"Yes."

He threw back the covers. "You probably have a concussion," he said, standing. He walked past her, an obvious limp making him no less threatening. As if the strength of his body wasn't enough to intimidate her, he towered over her like few men in her life ever had. He was six-five, easily, maybe more.

He walked back into the room, placing a mixing bowl on the table beside her. "Just in case," he said. "How are you feeling, other than the nausea?"

"Like I got hit by a train."

"That's not far off. Can you lift your head?"

"Not without fireworks going off in my brain."

"Understandable, given what happened."

She swallowed hard against her dry throat, then realized with horror she was close to tears. Her lips began to shake. "What happened, exactly?" she asked.

"You don't remember?"

"No."

He reached to touch her, and she recoiled.

"I just want to see your head," he said.

She eyed him warily. "I'm fine."

"I'm not going to hurt you, Olivia."

"Who are you?"

"Trevor Hawkins. Hawk."

"Why did you bring me here, Trevor Hawkins?"

He furrowed his brow. "We were in an accident. I came around a blind curve in my truck and there you were, stuck in the snow, standing outside your car. It was too late for me to stop. The impact threw you and you hit your head, which was lucky because both cars caught fire."

She lifted her hand to her head tentatively. A large lump and a messy scab were tender to the touch. Her hair was filled with hard bits of blood. She thought of her sharp, nasty headache. The nausea and dizziness. "Why aren't we in the hospital?"

"My cell phone was in my car. I assume yours was, too, and the phone here is dead. I haven't been able to contact anyone."

She turned her gaze to the front window, instantly sorry for the movement. "What about a passing car?"

"There aren't any. Wouldn't surprise me if they closed the road. We're in the middle of a blizzard on Warsaw Mountain."

"Blizzard?"

"Yes. It's pretty bad." He stood, walking past her

toward a hallway, and she noted a tattoo on his bicep, an eagle and an anchor.

"They have to have a radio or a TV somewhere," he said.

Warsaw Mountain.

The name meant nothing to her. She lived in… in… God, *where did she live?*

He walked back into the room, fiddling with a small radio in his hands. His eyes met hers. "You look like you're going to cry," he said.

She opened her mouth to speak, but nothing came out. Was this man her enemy or her friend? She watched as the muscles of his arm flexed with each movement of his hands.

If he was her enemy, she didn't stand a chance.

Please, let him be my friend.

"I can't remember where I live," she said, her voice little more than a whisper. He met her eyes with his calm, steely stare, clearly waiting for her to continue. She took a deep breath. "I don't remember if I have a cat, or a dog. I don't know if I live alone," she dropped her eyes, "or with someone else. The first thing I remember is waking up this morning."

She felt herself begin to come apart. Her face crumpled. "What's happening to me?" she cried. Her hands were trembling and she took gasping breaths of air. She grabbed the bowl and vomited, horrified that he was there watching her be sick.

He moved to her and tucked her hair behind her ear, making her squirm away.

"It's okay," He said, touching her arm.

She pulled away from him and stood, cradling the bowl, her head reeling from the movement. "It is not okay! Nothing is okay. Everything is wrong. Who are you, anyway?"

"Trevor Hawkins."

"You said that already. I mean, who are you? Why did you bring me here?"

"I told you, there was an accident."

"Bullshit."

He narrowed his eyes and took a step toward her. "What do you think happened?"

She lifted her chin, her mind searching for a reason not to tell him the truth, and finding none. "I think you drugged me. You slipped something into my drink and you took me here against my will."

"Why would I do that?"

Blood flooded her cheeks, heat filling her face. "To take advantage of me." She forced her eyes to remain on his as his stare slipped lower, taking in her body with cool assessment.

"The women I sleep with don't have to be drugged, Olivia." He closed the distance between them.

What would she do if he tried to touch her, or worse?

He leaned down and picked up the bowl, his body

so close to hers she felt herself tremble.

"I was on my way to visit a friend. I rounded a corner and there you were. Your car was stuck in the snow." He walked past her and she exhaled the breath she'd been holding. The water ran in the kitchen, and she knew he was cleaning out the dirty bowl.

She felt dirty, too. Cold and dirty and confused and aching. "Where's the bathroom?" she called. "I want to take a bath."

"Down the hall on the left, but there's no hot water. I'll heat some on the stove for you."

She fingered the waffle weave of her pajamas. "Where are my clothes? I assume I wasn't wearing long johns in the middle of a blizzard."

"Your clothes have blood on them. I'll find you something clean to wear. There's a whole closet full of clothes that should fit."

She nodded, instantly grimacing, then walked into the dark hallway. Her control over her emotions began to slip. Her mind worked frantically to recall something—anything—from before the accident.

She locked the door behind her and leaned against it, instantly in a full-blown cry. It was as if her life had begun the instant she woke up. The pain was swirling through her, no longer focused just on her head but in her belly and back. A word hovered on the edge of her willingness to name it, a word more frightening than any she'd ever experienced.

Amnesia.

Everything she ever knew was gone. She had amnesia and she was stuck here with this overwhelming man who could scare the bejesus out of her one moment and wash out her vomit the next.

Slipping down the door, she landed on the floor with a thud. Footsteps could be heard coming toward the bathroom.

"Olivia, are you okay?"

She leaned back against the locked door. This wasn't happening. This awful day was nothing more than a bad dream, and she need only wake up to return to her regularly scheduled life. Her eyes drifted shut despite the pounding and Trevor calling her name. The noises seemed to get farther away, less urgent, as if they were calling for someone else.

A pleasant darkness overcame her senses, welcoming her in, and she slumped to her side.

CHAPTER 8

"**O**LIVIA!" T REVOR POUNDED on the bathroom door, every muscle in his body at the ready. She'd passed out, he was sure of it, and he needed to get in there fast. His mind imagined every hard surface in that bathroom, the hard thunk of bone on porcelain, and blood streaming down Olivia's face.

He tried the door, finding it locked. He'd have to break it down. "Stand back," he yelled, just in case she could hear him. "Get away from the door." There was no response, as he'd expected there wouldn't be. With a twist of his torso, he kicked in the door. It opened halfway before running into her thigh.

He entered and tapped her cheek repeatedly, calling her name and willing her to wake up.

Her eyes opened and slowly focused on him. "What are you doing?" she mumbled.

"Helping you."

"I don't need help. I need hot water so I can take a bath."

He ran a hand through his hair, sheer frustration bubbling to the surface. "You passed out."

"No."

"Yes, you did."

She bit her lip. "Maybe I just didn't want to talk to you."

"You're joking, right?" His eyes bored into hers, surprised to see they were green, not blue as he'd earlier thought.

"No." She raised her chin. "I feel like crap, I can't remember anything, and you're scaring the hell out of me."

He raised his eyebrows high. "I'm scaring you? You lock yourself in here with a concussion and a hundred and one things to bang your head on, then you don't answer me when I try to see if you're okay."

She grabbed the sink and got to her feet. "Oh, please. I'm perfectly fine." She pivoted on her heel and listed dramatically to one side.

Trevor swooped in to catch her. "Oh, you're fine, all right. Not a damn thing wrong with you."

She pushed at his chest. "I don't want you to touch me!"

"I was keeping you from falling over."

"Let me go."

He released her and took a step back. "Just don't lock the door this time."

Olivia rubbed her arms as if to get rid of his touch. "If it will even close now that you pushed it in. Talk about overkill. What are you, some kind of macho policeman or something like that?"

"Something like that. I'll go check on your water."

"Do you want to nail the window shut before you go, just in case I try to escape?"

He crossed his arms. "Olivia, you're free to leave here anytime you want. I'm not holding you against your will. But there's a storm raging out there and no shelter for miles—if you can even find it—so I think you'd be better off hanging out with me for the time being."

Her bottom lip trembled and her voice cracked. "You might want to stop breaking down doors so you don't scare me to pieces."

She looked so young, so frightened. "I'm sorry. I didn't think…"

She held up a hand. "It's okay."

Damn it all, she was crying, her face crumpling up and her mouth pulling down hard.

"Oh, sweetheart," he said, "come here." He reached for her, but she stayed where she was, eyeing him warily until he dropped his arms. "I'm not going to hurt you," he said.

"I'm going to ask you something, and I want you to

tell me the truth. Did you drug me last night?"

"Absolutely not."

She bit her lip. "My head hurts. I can't remember anything…about last night, and when I woke up, you were…your body was…you were sleeping really close to me."

When you woke up, I was halfway to a boner from your sweet ass rubbing against my cock.

From the flush on her face, she remembered that part clearly. He'd better stick to the facts. "I did not drug you. We were in an accident and you hit your head. I brought you here and I slept next to you to keep you warm."

She nodded slowly.

"Olivia, I would never take advantage of a woman."

"Never?"

"Never."

"I hope that's true." She reached for the door, gesturing for him to leave. "Because as of this moment, you're the only person in the whole wide world I can remember." She closed the door between them.

CHAPTER 9

*H*OLY FUCK.

Gallant stared at the smoking, twisted metal at the bottom of the ravine. There was no way anyone could have survived this accident, and he cursed Brooke for taking off on her own and doing this to him.

What had possessed her? Like she didn't have it good enough already, famous and in demand and about to marry one of the richest men in the world?

And he liked her, damn it. A lot more than he'd liked the others. That was the kicker.

He moved toward the tangle of steel barely recognizable as Brooke's car, dreading the grisly find that awaited him. Maybe it was good that she was dead, that way Marco wouldn't kill her for running off before the wedding like she did.

Or make me do it.

The driver's seat was crushed but clearly empty. He moved around to the other side of the car. "What the hell?" From this angle it was obvious there were two cars in this tangle, not just one. He looked in what was left of the passenger compartments of both vehicles.

They were empty.

His cell phone rang and he sighed when he saw Johnson's name on the caller ID.

Fuck.

"She was in an accident," Gallant said. "I tracked her on the GPS through a fucking blizzard to the bottom of Warsaw Mountain. My Hummer barely made it down here, and it's still snowing. Her car and somebody else's are all crashed and burned up, but nobody's here."

"You really fucked up this time, Gallant."

He thought of the big blonde intern he'd screwed from SNL. Brooke had set them up, even told him he could use her dressing room, then she'd disappeared. He'd kept the intern out of his version of events when he broke the news to Johnson.

"Hey, I was supposed to keep her safe, not keep her from running off," he said.

"No, you were supposed to keep her in your sight at all times. If Marco finds out about this…"

"You didn't tell him?"

"There's no reason to tell him until we find her."

"But the wedding…"

"Isn't for almost two weeks. She couldn't have gotten far without transportation. Find her."

The wind blew, making Gallant shiver. Sometimes he hated this job. "What about me? I need transportation, too, you know. There's four feet of fucking snow on the ground."

"Fine. I'll leave a snowmobile outside the compound for you. Keep me posted, but be discreet."

"I can do that."

CHAPTER 10

WHILE OLIVIA BATHED, Hawk took inventory of the house. The snowshoes on the wall seemed to be real and functional. There were cross-country skis, boots, and poles in the bedroom closet. An assortment of household chemicals and alcohol that could be used to make Molotov cocktails, as well as some basic explosive components in the garage. There was also a snowmobile that ran, but it had so little gas it barely registered.

He came inside and sat on the bed, staring at the small pile of clothes in the corner and wondering if he'd made a mistake. Olivia had asked where her clothes were, and that was a perfect time to give them to her, bride T-shirt and all, but he didn't want to do it, which reminded him of the diamond he had in his pants pocket.

He pulled it out and stuck it on the tip of his index finger. It was too showy, too elaborate for the straightforward woman in the bathtub. He'd gotten her hot water, averting his eyes when he pulled back the curtain to add it to her bath.

It was an oddly intimate act.

Maybe it was because she looked so young, and he was feeling very protective of her after what they'd been through together, but he didn't want her to find out she was engaged before she could even remember where she lived.

Or at least that's what he was telling himself.

Something about her had snagged his interest. She was assessing him, considering whether or not he was worthy of her trust. He was a Navy SEAL, for God's sake, a member of the elite HERO Force. That made him one of the good guys, no matter how black his soul felt under her questioning stare.

Maybe if I hold on to her tightly, she can make me good again.

Where the hell had that thought come from?

She's engaged to someone else, and you have no business even thinking about this shit right now. You need to get to Steele.

Every step in Trevor's carefully laid plan had crashed to the ground when his car ran into hers. He'd been prepared for any eventuality—or so he thought— well stocked with weapons, ammunition, explosives, and all the tools he'd need to get in and out of Steele's compound without being caught. Now all he had taken for granted hung in the balance. He couldn't let the accident ruin his carefully laid plans.

He pressed his thumb onto the prongs holding the diamond, surprised to find them sharp like thorns. That thing was more than jewelry. It was a weapon, for chrissake. He couldn't help but wonder about the man who picked it out.

She could be marrying a serial killer. It's none of your business.

The song on the radio ended and the newscaster came on. "We're in for it tonight, folks. Snow will be completely changing over to freezing rain by morning, continuing for the next twenty-four hours before changing back to snow. The state's structural engineers have voiced some concerns about Warsaw Bridge's ability to handle the excess weight of an ice storm, and the bridge is closed to traffic through Thursday. The bridge is scheduled to be demolished and replaced in early spring."

Olivia's voice came from behind him. "The weather doesn't sound good. Do you think they'll get the roads cleared before all hell breaks loose?"

"No way." Hawk folded the ring in the palm of his hand and stood, turning to face her.

She wore the plaid pajama pants and a too-big T-shirt he'd brought her, her hair wet and her nipples standing out against the fabric. He forced his eyes to stay focused on hers. "Did you have a good bath?"

She frowned. "Not really. I couldn't stop trying to picture my own life, where I live—stuff like that—but no matter how hard I tried, there was nothing there."

He touched her arm, an electric tingle shooting up his hand, but this time she didn't pull away. "It will come. Give it time."

"Not like we're going anywhere soon." She brushed by him, the scents of woman, soap, and shampoo crowding him in the small space, and he closed his eyes. He could get lost in that smell if he allowed himself.

"And I wouldn't know where to go, either," she said. "Where do you go when you don't know who you are or where you belong?"

He didn't have amnesia. He knew where he had to go. He was stuck on this mountain and so was Steele.

So go and get him. Do what you came here to do.

His mind began to race. He needed a coat, some kind of weapon, and a way up the mountain. From the contents of the dresser, he knew there were clothes from a man similar in size to him.

"Trevor, thank you for everything you've done for me," she said, snapping his attention back to the present.

"You don't think I drugged you anymore?"

"No, but I do want to see my car."

He imagined it at the bottom of a ravine, its

charred steel frame like a skeleton in the snow. "It's too far away."

"It can't be that far if we walked here."

"You didn't walk. I carried you." She met his eyes and he shrugged one shoulder. "You were unconscious."

She frowned. "But how far…"

"About a mile."

"You carried me for a mile?"

"Maybe more."

She blew out air. "I find that hard to believe. No offense."

"None taken."

She frowned. "I really want to see my car."

"You can't. At least two feet of snow has fallen since then, and with that kind of hike, you'd be putting yourself in danger. Your concussion makes it dangerous for you to push yourself too far."

"Trevor, I just want to see that you're telling the truth, that I got here because of a car accident."

"You got here because of a car accident. You're just going to have to trust me."

"And if I don't like that answer?"

"I guess that's just too bad, Olivia." He ran a hand through his hair. "Listen, I need to go out and find some gasoline."

"What? Where?"

"There's a snowmobile in the garage, but no gas.

I'm going to go look for some."

She crossed her arms over her chest. "You think there's a gas station on the corner?"

"I'll find another vehicle. A lawn mower. Anything."

"The snow will be up to your waist."

"Not quite." He gestured to the wall above the fireplace. "But those are real snowshoes, so it doesn't matter."

"How long will you be gone?"

"I'll make sure you have plenty of wood for the fire before I go. There's enough food here for several weeks, if not longer."

"Whoa, wait. You're just going to leave me here?"

"I have to. I have things I need to do, and you seem like you're feeling better."

"But apparently, you've lost your freaking mind. We're stranded in the middle of a blizzard on an all-but-deserted mountaintop, and you're going to use the snowshoes from the living room wall—which were probably made in China and sold in some home decor store, by the way—to go hiking by yourself in search of gasoline?"

He narrowed his eyes. "'All-but-deserted mountaintop? How do you know where we are?" He walked toward her.

"I don't. That's the point. You can't leave me here all by myself." She touched his arm. "Please."

He took in her sweet, smooth complexion and her damp, curling hair. Not as young as he thought, just unusually beautiful. His gaze slipped lower, trailing along the neckline of the T-shirt, and watched the quickening rise and fall of her chest. His hands ached to touch her skin, to see if she was as soft as she looked. And that smell. The smell of her was so strong here, rising up from her neck with the warmth of her body.

Olivia's eyes were wide, and he stared into them, mesmerized as they dilated. He clenched his fists to keep from reaching for her, his chest and his hips and his face all sensitized for her touch, waiting. A rosy flush settled across her chest and neck, spreading to her cheeks, an answering excitement brewing in his belly.

Her stare dropped to his mouth, almost begging him to kiss her.

She licked her lips. "Please, Trevor."

She wasn't talking about him leaving.

Just one kiss.

It was a bad idea. The worst idea he'd ever had, and even as he acted on it, he knew it was the wrong thing to do. This woman was engaged to someone else and didn't remember. He pulled back just before their lips connected, sanity stepping in at the last moment, but she reached up and pulled him back down.

Her lips were full and soft and open beneath his, an invitation for more that he couldn't resist. His tongue moved into her mouth and she pressed herself against his length, her breathy sound of pleasure mixing with his own.

Her fingers were in his hair, her nails lightly scratching his scalp, and the sensation was amazing. Trevor rested his forehead on hers, his breath coming quickly.

"Don't leave me alone," she whispered.

He wanted to stay with her. That was the problem. Was he so easily sidetracked from the mission he'd dedicated himself to? He dropped his hands. "Olivia…"

"I'm scared." She crossed her arms again. "I won't apologize for that."

"There's nothing to be afraid of. You'll have food, clothing, and shelter for as long as you need it."

She met his eyes and he could see she was about to cry. "You're the only person I know in the whole world. If you leave…"

I won't have anyone.

Guilt reached up and pulled him down.

"Forget it," she said, waving her hands as she moved away. "You're right. I don't need you. I'm a big girl and I can take care of myself."

The war between his two responsibilities wrestled in his stomach like a rotten meal. It wasn't just her physical well-being he needed to account for, it was her mental health, as well. He had to admit, the idea of being so completely alone as she would be without him here was a frightening prospect indeed.

Damn it all to hell.

"Fine. Just give me a few hours. Let me find fuel."

She looked worried, and he could feel his plans slipping out of reach. He needed more than a few hours. He needed to be gone for as long as it took. "Maybe more."

She was trying to pretend she was okay with that, he could see it in her eyes and the way she shrugged one shoulder. "Fine."

His conscience nagged at him. He moved to the fire, stoking the embers and turning the logs. It was his fault she'd been hurt and was stranded in the woods without her car or cell phone, but damned if he would give up the first chance he'd had to get Steele since Ralph's death.

Trevor clenched his jaw, his eyes shooting to the window and the raging storm beyond. He'd planned months for this mission, practiced how to accomplish his goal alone. Now he was being sidetracked, and much as he knew he was being an asshole, he resented the diversion.

If he was going to get Steele, he had to do it before the weather cleared and the evidence drove right out from under his nose.

Eleven goddamn miles away, and it might as well be the other side of the world.

He flexed his shoulder and cracked his neck,

enough adrenaline coursing through his system to run to Steele's house and back in record time.

Run? On this knee? Who the fuck are you kidding?

From the location of the pain, he felt certain he'd either broken his patella or pulled a tendon, neither one of which was any good for running anywhere. Just walking on snowshoes in search of gasoline was going to hurt like hell and take ten times the energy it normally would have, but the end result was too important for him to forsake it. Trevor needed that snowmobile to get to Steele's compound.

But Olivia's well-being outweighed all that.

Damn it all to hell.

"Maybe I won't look for gas today. Maybe I'll just run up the road to the accident scene and see if I can find my jacket."

Or a gun.

Or any kind of weapon.

She met his eyes. "Thanks, Trevor."

The melodious sound of his name on her lips made his hand twitch, and he reminded himself she was spoken for.

Tell her. Tell her now.

She had a right to know everything he knew about her, at the very least. He opened his mouth, the bride shirt and engagement ring hanging on the tip of his tongue.

But she was fragile. Unsteady. She needed time to

get back on her feet before he told her about those things.

You're just afraid it will bring her whole memory back.

She cocked her head. "Everything all right?"

"Yeah. Everything's fine. I shouldn't be gone too long."

CHAPTER 11

OLIVIA STARED OUT the frosted window pane to the swirling scene beyond. Somewhere out there was her life, the people who knew her and the things she cared about. Had anyone even realized she was missing? Did she have family and friends concerned about her whereabouts, or was she as lonely in her forgotten life as she was in this limbo?

At least there was Trevor, though she sensed he was lying to her about his real reason for being here. She'd seen the way he was limping and knew he must be in considerable pain, so why venture out on foot?

Maybe his friend was a woman. A lover. The thought made her uncomfortable. But why shouldn't he have a lover? He was nothing to her, not even a friend. She pulled the sweater she'd found tighter around herself, the cut and style just slightly too small.

It was cold in the cabin despite the fire, and she wondered if he would suggest they sleep together for warmth as they had done the night before.

Surely it must have been for warmth.

She felt her cheeks flush. She might not remember the woman in the mirror, but she certainly remembered the pull between a woman and man, and there was one hell of a pull between them.

When they kissed, desire had spread through her like fire through dry kindling. She got so aroused, so quickly, she was shocked by her own reaction. Just thinking about it made her body come alive.

But she couldn't have affected him the same way. It was clear he wanted to get out of the cabin at the earliest opportunity, and it was his guilt over the accident that required him to stay. In her current state, she didn't care what kept him here, as long as something did.

Olivia sighed heavily and opened a cupboard, staring at cans of soup but seeing only Hawk's face inches from her own. She forced her eyes open wide. "Soup. Pick a can of soup, Livy."

She opened drawers and dusty cupboards, finding a can opener and pot and setting the soup on high. No one had been in this house in a long time, that was certain. She washed her hands, wondering when Trevor—Hawk—would be back.

It was an appropriate nickname for the man. He

paid attention. He'd caught her reference to the "all-but deserted mountaintop" before she caught it herself.

How the hell did I know that?

The hair on the back of her neck went up. Had she been in this area before? Did she live somewhere nearby? This remote location must be familiar to her in some way if she was making comments like that, yet nothing in this place seemed familiar at all.

She dried her hands on a dusty and yellowed towel, throwing it in the direction of the counter with a grimace. This cabin would be so nice if someone just gave it a once-over.

There were hardwood floors and high ceilings and strips of leaded glass in the windows, but any character it might have had was overshadowed by neglect.

Even the slightest bit of housekeeping would go a long way, and it would give her something to do besides look in the mirror and feel like she was losing her mind.

She began looking for cleaning supplies. Finding none, she wandered around until she discovered a broom closet near where she and Trevor kissed. She rested her head against the doorjamb, remembering the way his mouth had overpowered hers, lust coming quickly through her bloodstream like a drug.

It was a good thing he'd pulled away, because she'd been so caught up in her own fierce reaction to his kisses she'd wanted to ride that wave all the way onto the seashore. That was truly frightening. It was like an override switch on good judgment had been thrown the moment his lips melded with hers.

And they were stuck here—alone together—for the foreseeable future.

I made sure of that, didn't I?

The distinct smell of smoke made her head turn sharply, the nearly forgotten headache slamming into her skull with the motion. She ran back to the kitchen.

There, on the stovetop, was the yellowed kitchen towel, on fire. Without thinking, Olivia threw open a slender cupboard next to the range hood, knocked sugar and salt and spices out of the way, and withdrew a small fire extinguisher. She pulled the safety pin and sprayed the flames until nothing remained but the charred towel, covered in foam.

Her heart pounded.

She looked at the extinguisher in her hand as if it was a bloodied knife.

Her earlier words came back to her. ...*all-but-deserted mountaintop*...

"Oh my God. Oh my God," she chanted, her eyes jumping from the table to the refrigerator to the cupboard where she'd found the fire extinguisher.

Her mind was playing tricks on her, keeping secrets while she desperately needed the truth. "If you know this place, you'd better tell me now," she said to herself. "No more of this amnesia bullshit, Olivia."

She squeezed her eyes shut, willing her memories back into place, but none came. She opened her eyes. If she knew what was in one cabinet, maybe she knew what was in another. Her gaze went to the cupboard over the refrigerator, and she exhaled a shaky breath. "Pitchers, a big blue platter, baskets," she whispered, reaching for the handle as if it might be hot and burn her.

A ceramic blue platter.

Several baskets.

She moved them out of the way with shaking fingers. Two drink pitchers stood in the back of the cabinet.

Son of a bitch.

Trevor called from the great room. "Olivia?"

She slammed the cupboard door as he walked into the kitchen. "What?"

"Is something burning?"

"Not anymore." She crossed her arms over her chest. "I thought you left."

He narrowed his eyes. "The snowshoes don't fit right. I need some string or something." He moved to the stove. "What happened?"

"Just a little fire. It's okay." She waved her hand. "I accidentally put a kitchen towel on a hot burner."

"Is that foam from a fire extinguisher?"

She nodded. "Yep. Lucky thing I found it."

He leaned against the counter, and she wanted to

lean into him, to take from his strength and release her own weakness. He could take that from her, hold her up when everything she knew was falling backwards. She took a step back, noting the disappointment in his eyes and suspecting it matched her own.

"You okay?" he asked.

She longed to tell him the truth, confide in him that she'd clearly been here before and knew this place on some level. But hadn't he only agreed to stay with her because of her memory loss? She was helpless, and he was clearly a helper. If her memory returned, he'd be gone faster than she could say run.

No, she would keep this new discovery to herself, at least until there was something more important to share than baskets and a fire extinguisher. "I'm fine. Just a little freaked out by the fire."

"I don't blame you. It's all right now." He gestured toward the hallway. "I'm going to go look in the garage. I think I saw some twine in there."

"Good luck." She watched as he turned and walked away, confident she'd made the right decision.

CHAPTER 12

MARCO ACERO CROSSED one Italian leather loafer over the other and tugged on his French cuff. "Frankly, Señor Alvarez, it doesn't matter what you want."

The gray-haired man across the table tapped his gold pen on his palm, a fine sheen of sweat on his brow. "My people are prepared to make you a fair settlement."

"The goods have been bought and paid for, and there will be no bickering at this point in the negotiations."

"These are not negotiations. This is thievery."

Acero smirked. "Semantics."

"You are nothing but a common thief!"

The intercom in the middle of the conference table beeped. "Bella Grayson's on the phone, sir."

His lips tightened into a firm line.

"You can put it through, Helen. Mr. Alvarez and I are finished." He waited while the older man left the room, then stared at the phone, wondering what Bella could want. If there were a way to find out without speaking to the bitch, he'd do it in a heartbeat.

Once he and Brooke were married, he planned to push Bella out of his wife's life completely. His eyes went to a high shelf, three gold statuettes glittering back at him. For now, he would put on a show worthy of Brooke's Emmy Awards. He pressed the button on the phone.

"Hello, Bella! Did you see your sister's fine performance on Saturday Night Live this weekend?"

"I caught part of it."

"The ratings are through the roof. Everyone tuned in to find out who Brooke Barrons will be marrying."

"Let me guess. She didn't tell them."

"You keep the public's interest by withholding the information they want."

"Riiighht. Listen, Olivia was supposed to pick me up at the airport in Denver yesterday, but she didn't come. I keep calling her, but I just get her voice mail."

Denver? He narrowed his eyes. "So call Gallant."

"I did. He said she sent him home Saturday night after the show. Told him his services weren't required."

He swore colorfully in Spanish. "She said she

wouldn't do that again."

And Gallant should fucking know better, but that's another conversation.

"But my sister doesn't belong to you, and she doesn't always want your goons following her around."

"My employees keep her safe."

"Your employees smother her independence."

He looked at the golden clock on his desk. "Why did you wait so long to contact me?"

"Because I don't like you, and if she took some time off to reconsider becoming your wife, then that seemed like a good thing. But now I'm worried."

"So it's me you turn to, because you know I will find her. You say I don't care for her, but I am the only one taking care of her."

"Bullshit…"

Marco hung up the phone and brought his finger to his mouth, biting down hard on the nail. He'd given Brooke everything she ever wanted and then some. He'd facilitated her fame and hired the staff who created the incomparable Brooke Barrons out of a tomboy named Olivia Grayson, who wore dirty sneakers and cut-off jeans.

That was the easy part. Making her fall in love with him had been more of a challenge. But Brooke had a weakness, an insecurity he had twisted to his advantage.

The woman hated to be alone.

He'd simply taken away the people she loved, and she had come running to him like a hungry puppy.

She was his now.

Bella hadn't taken care of her sister! If she had, Brooke never would have agreed to marry him. He stopped biting his nails and dialed the phone. He had too much invested in Brooke to loose her now.

CHAPTER 13

A N HOUR LATER, the dust in the cabin remained untouched as Olivia searched for memories. With Trevor gone, she was free to explore without him suspecting she was familiar with the cabin. Drawer after drawer, she rifled through generic clothing and possessions, nothing giving a clue as to its owner.

Exhausted and frustrated, she flopped face-up on the queen-sized bed and stared at the ceiling. There, in the corner of the room, was a framed-out rectangle that could only be the access to the attic.

"How did I miss this?" she mumbled, pulling down a slender handle and exposing a compact ladder. She eagerly reached up to extend it, and froze.

An image appeared in her mind, her own hand on this ladder, tucking it and the access door away. A tremendous sadness filled her spirit at the memory.

What was up here that could make her feel so empty inside? She searched her mind for the answer, just as she'd done with the kitchen cupboards.

Everything.

A chill went up her spine. It was dark, and she grabbed a flashlight she'd found before venturing up the ladder with cautious footsteps. Poking her head into the attic, she shined the light in a circle. The space was small and half the height of a normal room, with a stack of boxes on one end, the smell of old newspapers and stale air making her wrinkle her nose.

Settling next to the pile, she pulled down the first box. "Pictures" was scribbled in marker across the top, and she felt her stomach tighten as she opened the box and pulled away the newspaper wrapped around a frame.

A middle-aged man had his arms around two smiling girls in their graduation caps and gowns. One of those girls was her.

She covered her mouth.

Her eyes glazed over as she remembered…

She was in a car, driving in that too-fast reckless way you always had to drive to get up Warsaw Mountain in the snow, when she suddenly feared she'd missed her turn and slowed down the slightest bit—just enough to lose momentum and the traction of her tires on the road.

Then she was stuck, cursing as she tried to push the

car on the snow-covered roadway, the wind from the storm howling in her ears. That must have been when Trevor hit her. She never would have heard him coming in that storm.

He'd been telling the truth.

She picked up the graduation picture again, touching the face of the man and the girl, feeling her throat tighten. Ellie and Frank. She held the picture to her chest.

This place didn't just happen to be close to the accident scene. This had been her destination all along. Her breathing got faster as the realization sliced through her new reality. "I was coming here. I had to get something…to find something…"

Her head began to ache as she concentrated. She could remember the urgency, the importance of her journey, but could not for the life of her remember what it was. "Damn it, Olivia," she said out loud. "What were you looking for, and why was it so important that you had to drive through a blizzard to find it?"

CHAPTER 14

TREVOR PUT ON the snowshoes, grabbed a shovel he'd found in the garage, and took off down the driveway. It was snowing as if it would never stop, and he pulled his hood over his head as he limped through the snow. He took his time, babying his knee, testing to see which positions could hold weight as his mind replayed his kiss with Olivia in one continuous, torturous loop.

The walk was punishing, and he was a man who needed punishment. He had no right to take the kisses she offered, not when he was keeping the most basic information about her life a secret. Worse yet, he knew he'd be hard-pressed to deny himself if and when she offered him more.

You're a fucking bastard.

With every step, his thoughts of Olivia grew more

inappropriate. Fantasy stepped in where reality left off, the race of his imagination a welcome distraction from his physical discomfort.

When he rounded the corner onto the main road, the mailbox was nowhere in sight. It had been completely covered in snow. He looked around him at the woods, noting two distinctive trees to mark the turn, and headed for the accident scene, the downward slope of the road causing his knee to catch and grind.

A noise echoed in the distance and he froze, his eyes narrowing. It sounded mechanical, possibly an engine of some sort. He stood still, his ears carefully listening for several minutes. Could it be a snowplow, come to free them from their isolation? Or a helicopter in the sky, searching for the missing Olivia? Surely her fiancé was aware of her location and that she didn't get wherever she'd been heading, which could pose one hell of a problem for Trevor if that fiancé of hers came looking for her here.

Hawk couldn't afford to be seen on Warsaw Mountain.

Olivia already knows you're here.

He cursed out loud.

Steele's death was bound to make headlines. How would he keep Olivia from turning him in? He shook his head. He'd deal with that when he had to.

He stopped walking and listened hard for the sound for several seconds. It seemed to have stopped.

Rounding the wide corner before the accident scene, it felt as if he was going further back in time than twenty-four hours, as if the accident had been days or weeks earlier, as if he'd known Olivia longer and been sidetracked from his mission far longer than he really had.

Several small drifts of snow remained close to the crash site, and Trevor began digging with the shovel. Drift after drift proved to be exactly that—a formation of snow caused by the wind.

He was just about to give up when his shovel caught on something solid. He dug out a suitcase, one side of it charred and dented from the blast. Beneath it was a long, white plastic garment bag emblazoned with Beverly Hills Bridal in silver letters.

He hadn't found his coat, but he'd managed to find Olivia's wedding dress.

Great.

He had to take the dress and the suitcase with him. He owed her that much, but given that he hadn't told her she was engaged, the dress was bound to be an awkward discovery. Draping the garment bag over his arm and picking up the case, he was nearly back to the cabin when the same mechanical sound caught his attention once more.

This time, he was sure it was a snowmobile, the rise and fall of the engine's purr now easily familiar. There was someone else on this mountain. Someone with transportation and gasoline. Hopefully it was a kindly neighbor, but he couldn't discount the possibility it was one of Steele's men.

He began to move more quickly, tuning out the sensations from his knee. He had to find the snowmobile's tracks, had to trace them back to their source so he could find gasoline to get to Steele.

Hawk was nearly back to the cabin's drive when he found the tracks, two parallel lines in the snow that meant he would be able to kill Steele after all.

"Booyah!" he exclaimed. He'd wanted this for years, hundreds of days spent planning to get the man responsible for Ralph's death, and with a snowmobile he knew he could do it.

The snowmobile's tracks suddenly reversed direction. Trevor furrowed his brow as he followed them up the hill with his eyes. The rider had changed direction and turned back to follow Trevor's tracks.

The snowmobile was heading toward the cabin.

Adrenaline shot through Hawk's system. His mind began to race. He'd left Olivia alone. Alone and vulnerable, even though he knew they were close to Steele's compound.

It could be a neighbor who saw the smoke from our fire and wants to make sure we're okay.

But as a Navy SEAL, he'd learned to trust his instincts, and his instincts were screaming that she was not safe. His breath came in heavy pants. He followed the tracks within sight of the cabin and as they veered in a wide arc around the tree line. Whoever was driving that snowmobile was scouting, just as he himself would have done, then the tracks disappeared into the woods.

Was the rider staring back at him from the trees, hidden from view, or was he truly gone?

He had to see if Olivia was okay before investigating further. He ran inside, throwing the garment bag and suitcase into the garage. "Olivia?" he called. "Olivia!"

"Here, I'm down here," came the answer, and he bolted down the hall toward her. Just as he entered the room and caught a glimpse of her dusting, the sound of a snowmobile's engine roared to life right outside the cabin walls, making them jump.

"Get down!" he yelled, tackling her. "Stay away from the windows!"

She did as she was told, cowering on the floor. He had to get a weapon. He stayed low, quickly getting to the kitchen and yanking open a kitchen drawer. He selected a seven-inch knife, its blade gleaming, and his mind flashed back to Ralph on the floor of Steele's warehouse, gagging on his own blood as he begged Steele for his life.

Steele would not have another chance to hurt someone else Trevor cared about. He took another knife out and slammed the drawer shut. His heart was hammering in his chest now, a steady rhythm beating like a warrior's drum.

He walked back to the bedroom and began rifling through the closet. The snowshoes had been awkward. He needed something faster and had spotted just the thing when he inventoried the cabin.

She asked from the floor, "What's going on, Trevor? Who was that outside?"

Her plaintive voice pawed at him as he flipped through heavy coats and brightly colored parkas. One had ski goggles attached to the hanger.

She pulled at his arm. "Talk to me, damn it! Who was that out there?"

"I don't know."

"Why don't I believe that?"

He stopped and met her glassy eyes. "I'm telling the truth." Trevor turned back to the closet. "There's nothing to be scared about." He caught sight of something shiny in the back of the closet and forced the hanging clothes apart.

There, on the back wall, were the several sets of cross-country skis he'd been looking for. He pulled them out, along with poles and boots. "I'm just going to catch up to that person and see if I can get some gasoline."

"But you told me to get down," she said. "To get away from the windows, like someone was shooting at us."

He forced his foot into a too-tight snow boot and looked at her like she was hallucinating. "No one was shooting at us."

"Trevor! Stop bullshitting me!"

He turned back to the closet, searching for gloves and deciding what to say.

"I don't know who was on that snowmobile, but I don't have a good feeling about them, and I'm going after them to see what I can find out."

She looked from his ski boots up to his face. "You can't possibly catch him."

"I think I can."

She narrowed her eyes. "Who are you?" she whispered.

"Former Navy SEAL officer Trevor Hawkins, current lieutenant commander of HERO Force Alpha Squad. Put the fire out and the lights off until I know what we're dealing with. Take this knife and keep it with you at all times."

She looked at the blade in her hand and took a step backward.

He zipped up his parka and pulled the goggles over his eyes, then slipped out the door without another word.

CHAPTER 15

O LIVIA HADN'T MOVED since Trevor left.
       Navy SEAL.

Lieutenant Commander.

HERO Force.

No wonder he looked like a warrior. That's exactly what he was.

Even wounded, she believed him when he said he could catch up to the man on the snowmobile, physics be damned. The rules of motion hadn't been formally introduced to Trevor Hawkins.

She'd only known him for a short time, but she was in awe of this man. He was physically and emotionally strong, and he took care of her. Chasing after the guy on the snowmobile came as no surprise.

Trevor was a man who would protect her.

Olivia frowned. Somehow she knew she needed

protecting, though from what, or whom, she couldn't imagine. There was a fatigue in her bones that held its own memories, and it stood witness to hard times in her past and a lingering sadness she couldn't explain.

Trevor had crashed into her world, and her history had been wiped clean. Maybe that was no accident. Maybe the strength of his character had scared her reality away.

You're being melodramatic, and you're getting too attached to a man who's only bound to you by the weather.

Where would he go if he were able to leave? Now that she knew what he did for a living, she wondered if he was on a mission. She blew out air at the cloak-and-dagger word. *Mission.* Did anyone really go on missions?

He works for a group called HERO Force, and you're making fun of the word mission?

Seriously.

Or maybe he really was here to see a woman.

A lover.

She crossed her arms. A man like that could have whatever woman he wanted, and he no doubt did.

"That's one lucky lady," she said, then sighed. His body alone! Add to that, he was a protective, kind, Navy SEAL, and the women must be falling all over themselves to get to him. If she were available, she certainly would be.

Her eyes popped open wide.

If she were available?

Goose bumps swept up her arms, but no more thoughts came, no picture of a man she should be missing. She should be thrilled at the slightest glimpse of her memory returning, but the contrast between her thoughts of Trevor and the unsettled feeling in the pit of her stomach at the idea of the real man in her life was alarming.

She wandered through the darkening cabin. The fire was nearly out, but she put down her knife and used the fire poker to spread out the remaining coals before taking a seat by the window. Snow was falling softly against the luminous purple sky, the entire landscape covered in white, and glowing. He was out there somewhere, tangling with something neither of them understood, and she hoped he would come home soon.

Home? This isn't home!

As soon as the roads were open, Hawk would go back to his life, and she would be left to fend for herself.

Maybe by then she'd have her memory back.

Or maybe I don't even want it.

Her shoulders shook, whether from cold or her thoughts, she wasn't sure. It was certainly cold in the cabin, and bound to get a lot colder. She thought of Trevor keeping her warm, a silently ticking clock counting down their time together until she would be without him and alone.

"I don't want to remember my real life," she whispered, surprising herself with the truth in her own statement. "Please don't make me remember," she begged to the empty room.

CHAPTER 16

D USK COLORED THE landscape purple and pink as Trevor set out on his skis. The motion of his cross-country stride was easier on his knee than the snow shoes had been, and he followed the snowmobile's tracks in good time. As he feared, they led up the mountainside toward Steele's compound, leaving little doubt as to the other man's employer, if not identity.

The tint of his goggles was too dark, and he pushed them up onto his forehead. This would be a difficult ski with the benefit of daylight. Without it, he knew his ability was limited, but he continued to follow the tracks. Even though getting back to the cabin would be far faster than this trip away from it, he calculated he only had a few more minutes before he would need to turn around.

Up ahead, a large boulder was silhouetted against

the midnight-blue sky. Hawk detected the faint smell of hot metal in the air, markedly different than the crisp forest breeze.

It was the smell of an engine that had recently been running.

His mysterious snowmobiler was nearby, hoping to escape detection, which made Hawk that much more certain this was not just a friendly neighbor out for a joyride. Hawk slowed his stride, careful not to look like he was stopping, as his eyes swept back and forth.

The boulder was the most likely spot for an ambush. As Hawk closed the distance between it and him, he readied himself for the attack. He'd only have a split second to disarm the other man.

Just as he passed the boulder, a fist reached out from behind it, heading straight for his jaw. Trevor grabbed it in midair, twisting it back before slamming it on the boulder. The man let out a pained grunt as a handgun flew out of his grip and over the boulder.

"You don't know when to quit, do you?" asked the man, his voice muffled behind his helmet.

"Are you talking to me, or yourself?" Trevor punched the other man in the solar plexus.

The squawk of a walkie-talkie came from the snowmobile. "Gallant, do you copy?"

Recognition slammed through Hawk. The most awful image appeared in his brain, a visceral memory so ingrained in his mind he could have been standing there today.

Ralph on the floor, bloodied and beaten but still fighting back against the big man who answered to Steele. "*Gallant, that's enough. Tie his hands and feet, then get me my hunting knife.*"

The man from the snowmobile had the same physique as the man in Hawk's memory, and the muscles in Hawk's body became supercharged with adrenaline. He grabbed Gallant, ripping off his helmet, dominating the other man with his strength born of emotion. There was the face Hawk remembered. "You!"

Hawk was going to kill Steele, but first he was going to kill this guy.

Gallant struggled to be free, but Hawk threw him against the boulder with such force, Gallant's head hit the stone with a sickening thud. He was stunned for a half second, then rallied and fought again. Hawk elbowed him in the chin as he once again forced the big man against the boulder.

This time when his head hit the rock, he went down.

The radio squawked again. "Gallant, are you there?"

Hawk stared at the man on the ground and assessed the threat he posed. Gallant was either dead, out cold, or faking, but he wouldn't get far in the seconds it would take Hawk to answer the man on the radio. He turned and picked up the receiver. "Copy."

The slightest noise behind him had him whipping back around, just as Gallant rolled over the edge of the cliff.

Hawk dropped the radio and ran to the precipice. It was too dark to see if the other man was dead or had escaped. Hawk cursed under his breath.

The voice on the radio asked, "Any sign of our runaway?"

Trevor hurried back to the snowmobile. "Negative."

"Fuck." The man sighed heavily. "This is not good. I'll leave the utility gate open for you and Johnson. Park the snowmobiles off-site, sleep in the galley, and try again in the morning."

"Copy that." Trevor moved back to the edge of the cliff, but it was impossible to see how far down it went or what had become of Gallant. At least Hawk had gotten the snowmobile and radio, even if the other man had managed to escape.

Hawk took off his skis and bungeed them to the snowmobile as his mind repeated the man on the walkie-talkie.

Utility gate.

Sleep in the galley.

Johnson.

These were Steele's men, and they were looking for someone.

Any sign of our runaway?

One of the women Steele was holding must have managed to escape. A gust of icy wind blew through the trees and he hoped the woman was able to find shelter. Without it, she wouldn't survive long enough to find freedom or be recaptured.

The thought reminded him of Olivia.

If you had a shred of decency, you'd put her on the snowmobile with you and take her back to Denton in the morning, where she belongs.

The thought made him still.

He would have enough gas to make it down the mountain, but not enough to make it back up, and refueling now would bring attention to himself. Hell, even finding a place for Olivia to stay would do that, effectively squashing his plans to kill Steele.

You could take Olivia to Denton, then come back and rescue the women. You just wouldn't be able to kill Steele.

Ralph's killer would go free.

He ground his teeth and started the engine, carefully winding his way back to the cabin in the moonlight. He couldn't do it. He didn't know if that made him a better man or a worse one.

There had to be payback, had to be revenge. He couldn't let Ralph die in vain, Ralph's child grow up without a father while Steele continued on with business as usual.

CHAPTER 17

TREVOR HAD BEEN gone too long, and it was nearly dark outside. What if he couldn't find his way back without the chimney smoke to guide him? Olivia paced the living room, questioning whether or not she should go after him. Getting herself lost on this mountain wasn't going to help anyone, and she was damn sure she didn't know how to ski.

She lit a candle and made her way to the bedroom. Opening the closet, she flipped through coats, jackets, and snow pants. Nearly everything here belonged to a man, though she supposed she could wear something too big if she had to.

Suddenly, she froze, the hair on the back of her neck standing up. She was overwhelmed by the sensation that she was being watched, and wished she'd thought to close the drapes. Forcing her hand to move, she continued to flip hangers.

What if the snowmobile guy got away from Trevor, and now he's come back for me?

Or maybe it is Trevor.

No. Trevor wouldn't be peeking in through the window.

Her heart was racing and a high-pitched hum invaded her hearing. This was fight or flight, with nowhere to go and nothing to fight with.

Think, Olivia. Think.

Damn it, where had she put that knife? Her mind flew through the cabin, looking for anything that could help her. Another kitchen knife, but they were too far away. A metal shovel that had caught her eye in the garage, also too far.

The baseball bat under the bed.

She closed her eyes, seeing it clearly in her memory. A good ol' Louisville Slugger that was never intended for sports.

The slightest noise at the window confirmed her suspicions. Someone was out there, she was certain. Fear made her limbs stiff and difficult to move. If she was going to do this, she had one chance to do it right.

One, two, three!

Olivia blew out her candle and spun around, the room thrown into darkness. She dropped to the ground and crawled to the bed, making her way around it by feel and wishing her eyes would adjust so she could see.

Sure enough, her hand closed around the barrel of a baseball bat.

A noise came from the other room and she tiptoed down the hall, bat at the ready. She forced her fear to disconnect from her body. Her eyes adjusted to the lack of light and she rounded the corner into the living room.

The front door was open several inches, the sound of freezing rain falling outside like white noise. Olivia pulled the bat back over her shoulder and prepared to fight for her life.

CHAPTER 18

T REVOR ROUNDED THE corner into the drive, and the cabin came into view. Olivia had done as he asked, letting the fire go out so there was no sign of their presence, and he felt his shoulders relax.

There was something nice about coming back to her. He liked the way she'd confronted him when she thought he'd drugged her, and the way she'd felt in his arms when they kissed. He wanted to fight with her again and do some more kissing, maybe even at the same time.

He stashed the snowmobile inside the garage, then looked up at the still-swirling snow. The blizzard would be their cover, erasing their tracks and wiping the slate clean overnight.

Keeping them safe.

And alone together.

He chastised himself for his thoughts about Olivia. Whoever Gallant had been talking to was expecting the henchman back at Steele's mansion tonight. Whether Gallant returned on foot, injured from his fall off the cliff, or didn't return at all, that meant Hawk and Olivia had just inched one step closer to Steele's inner circle.

That should keep Hawk from thinking about Olivia's sweet body, but it didn't. He reached for the handle on the door of the house and found it ajar.

Hawk instantly went on alert, pulling out his knife as his mind raced to assess the situation. Gallant couldn't have gotten here before him, if he had survived the fall, which meant someone else was at the cabin.

He flashed back to the man on the walkie-talkie.

You and Johnson.

Johnson!

Damn it, there was more than one of Steele's men running around Warsaw Mountain, and Hawk had left Olivia alone.

He kicked open the door.

Something solid and heavy crashed into the wall beside him. He reached for it, recognizing the wooden barrel of a baseball bat and sliding down it to find his attacker's hands, quickly capturing them with his own.

They struggled, and Trevor recognized Olivia's all-too familiar scent. He used her hands to pull her toward him. "It's me." She continued to fight him. "It's me, Olivia!"

She stopped wrestling. "Trevor?"

"Yes."

"Oh, God." She fell into his arms, wrapping herself tightly around his torso. "I was so scared," she sobbed. "Someone was outside the window and I didn't know what was happening and all I could think to do was grab the baseball bat."

"Which window?"

"The back bedroom."

He took off along the side of the house, his knife at the ready, and rounded the corner. Sure enough, fresh snowmobile tracks came close to the back bedroom window. His eyes scanned the horizon and the forest that bordered the house on three sides, but he saw nothing unusual.

He continued around the house. The tracks could very well be Gallant's. Not enough snow had fallen to completely bury anything since then, but they could also be freshly made by someone else.

Like Johnson.

He went back inside. "There are no new tracks out there. Just the ones from before."

"Oh, gosh. I'm such an idiot." She hung her head. "I thought I was going to die and you would come back and find my body."

"Shh," he whispered gruffly as she babbled. "It's

okay now."

"I'm so glad you're back. I was scared. I would have sworn there was somebody outside that bedroom window, and then the front door was open…"

"You didn't do that?"

She shook her head. "No."

Maybe those tracks were made more recently, after all.

She went into his arms, resting her head on his shoulder.

He rubbed his hand down her silken hair, his lips naturally moving to hers to soothe her with gentle kisses. "I'm sorry you were scared."

"I thought I was going to die, and I was so glad that you'd been here with me, Trevor. That I haven't been alone."

He wanted to comfort her, wanted to pull her back into his arms like he had before. They'd already kissed once, which made it easier for him to do it a second time. He pressed kiss after kiss on her lips, each one gentler than the last. "I'm glad, too," he whispered.

His eyes had adjusted to the darkness and he could see hers in the dim light, questions shining in their depths. He took her mouth once more, none too gently this time, in an all-consuming lover's kiss.

She responded to him, kissing him back, and he twirled her around so that her back was to the wall, pinioning her there against him. He needed this, needed to feel her body against his and her mouth intimately melding with his mouth.

His hand reached up to her breast of its own accord, lightly cupping her there before he moved it back to her waist, but she took his hand back to her breast and squeezed it, and he kneaded her full, soft flesh as his hips bucked against hers.

He lifted his head, panting with the effort of holding back, even as she held his hips tightly to her. She was engaged to another man, a man she loved who—he was sure—she'd never knowingly betray.

He hated himself in that moment, hated himself for lying to her and wanting her anyway. He couldn't sleep with her while she didn't know who she was. He cupped her jaw with his hand and opened his mouth to speak.

"You'd better not say we shouldn't do this," she said, pressing her head against his head, her chest against his chest. "We don't have to sleep together, Hawk. Just be with me for a little while."

Trevor closed his eyes, sensations and temptation pulling him through the darkness. When she touched her lips to his once more, he exploded. His hands moved down, circling her neck and teasing her with his grip before reaching for the hem of her shirt and pulling it up to expose her voluptuous breasts.

That was the word for her. Voluptuous, with curves like the fierce waves of the ocean that begged to be fitted against him.

You swore you'd never take advantage of her.

Damn it, he knew that was a mistake the moment he'd said the words. She sucked lightly on his neck and his muscles clenched as he became overwhelmed with the desire to lower her to the floor and sink into her sweetness, to love her body with a ferociousness born of hot, slick lust.

He lifted his head from hers, nearly growling with the effort it took to do so. "We should stop."

"I don't want to." She went up on her tiptoes and kissed him with her full, tantalizing lips.

Every taste of her made him crazy for more, and he raked the gentle softness of her upper lip with his stubbled face, knowing he was scraping her and loving how she moaned out loud when he did it.

She would be an amazing lover, able to take his passion in kind, and he squeezed the flesh of her ass hard with both hands. She lifted one leg around his waist, pressing her most intimate spot against the fly of his jeans, and the heat of her sex radiated through his clothing.

"Tell me to stop, Livy," he ground out coarsely. "Tell me you want the life you can't remember more than you want me, or I won't be able to stop myself from fucking you."

She threw her head back. "I don't care…"

"Think!" He held her face, one hand on either side as he stared into her eyes in the near-darkness. "Is there someone you care about. Someone you…love?" He swallowed against the strain in his throat, the strain of his cock against his jeans. "Don't let me ruin your life so easily, damn it."

Olivia's eyes went wide and her leg dropped to the floor. "What do you mean?"

"I didn't tell you everything I know." He ran a hand through his hair.

She crossed her arms. "You're scaring me."

"You fell on your left side when you were thrown during the accident. Your hand was swelling up, and I had to take off your ring." He reached into his pocket and pulled out the diamond engagement ring, holding it out to her.

She stared at it. "I'm engaged?"

"Looks that way."

Out with it, Hawk.

He swallowed hard. "Your shirt said Bride."

Her head shot up. "You knew I was engaged and you didn't tell me?"

"I wanted you to remember on your own." It sounded indefensible when he said it out loud.

Hell, it is indefensible.

She took the ring from his hand. "It didn't keep you from kissing me."

"No. It didn't, and it should have. I'm sorry."

She turned away.

He forced his feet to be still and his arms to remain

at his sides when they wanted to go after her, reach for her. It was better this way. He had no right to this woman, no claim to her body or mind.

"You promised," she said quietly. "You promised you'd never take advantage of me."

"I know, and I'm sorry." He hated himself in that moment. He was the lowest of the low, the bottom of the barrel. "It was inexcusable."

"If we're being completely honest, I suspected," she said.

"That you were engaged?"

"That I wasn't free to be kissing you, yes."

He pursed his lips. He should let it go at that, but his mouth opened of its own accord. "Then why did you?"

She turned around to face him, her eyes dark. "For the same reason you did."

They stared at each other, the tension between them like the tightest wire. He swore he could still feel raw passion between them, as if her knowledge of her life outside of these walls changed nothing about their lives inside of them.

What would she do if he kissed her again? Would she push him away or pull him in tightly against her? He hated himself for even wondering, but the pull of sexual attraction would not be denied.

He cleared his throat. "I need to get the furnace working, or we're going to freeze to death tonight."

She nodded. "And I should find us something for dinner."

He moved for the basement door, then stopped and turned around. "Are you sorry it happened, Livy?"

She acted as though she didn't hear. She was just standing in the middle of the room staring into space, the ugly ring on the tip of her index finger.

CHAPTER 19

TREVOR LIT A candle and made his way down a narrow staircase to the basement, the smell of must making his nose twitch. The furnace was in the far corner near the electrical box, and as he moved toward it, a bright red tag on the exhaust pipe caught his eye.

WARNING: Cracked Heat Exchanger. Carbon Monoxide Hazard.

It was handwritten in thick black marker, signed with a scribble, and fastened to the furnace with a zip tie. He'd never seen anything like it.

He pried open the panel on the furnace. It was older, with a cylindrical heat exchanger, and he moved to a small workbench to locate some basic tools. Within minutes he was inspecting it in the candle's light. Sure enough, there was a crack.

"Son of a gun," he whispered. They wouldn't be getting any heat out of this furnace today. Carbon monoxide from the burning fuel would flow right out of the crack and into the cabin, killing anyone who slept in the house.

He laid on his back and stared up at the foreboding red tag. Who would leave something like this, instead of fixing the problem? It was potentially deadly and just sitting here waiting for someone to turn the gas back on and adjust the thermostat.

He ran his finger over the crack while his mind considered the possibilities, then inhaled quickly when his finger was sliced open by a sharp metal edge.

What the hell?

A cracked heat exchanger shouldn't have a sharp edge like that. No, the "crack" in this cylinder was only made to look like it was naturally occurring. In fact, it had been deliberately punctured with some kind of sharp tool.

Trevor sucked on his bleeding finger and made his way back upstairs. Olivia was standing in the kitchen, wiping her hands on a towel.

"Any luck on the furnace?" she asked.

"No." He told her about the sabotaged heat exchanger and explained what it meant. "Someone did this on purpose, to fill this place with carbon monoxide."

"Why would someone do that?" she asked.

"The only reason I can think of is murder."

She stared at him several beats too long, the color seeming to drain from her face.

"Olivia, are you okay?"

Her eyelids fluttered and he moved to grab her, catching her just as she went limp and passed out.

CHAPTER 20

J AX ANDERSSON BENT his six-foot-four frame and peered into a retinal scanner. A metal door opened to a long, lighted hallway and he entered with the heavy stomp of his military boot.

He took a sip of his coffee, the hot brew mixing with the acid in his stomach that had begun churning when he called Logan to have him track Hawk's cell phone.

He should have known the shit was going to hit the fan when Logan first told HERO Force about the intel that Steele was taking another shipment, more than a month ago. Hawk had gone ballistic, nearly lunging across the conference table. "This is our chance to get that son-of-a-bitch," he'd said, his eyes shining with eagerness.

Jax had matched Hawk's enthusiasm with a level

gaze. "No. The intel's unconfirmed. We can't dedicate our resources on some half-assed report that Steele's involved in human trafficking."

Hawk had stood up, meeting his stare. "It wouldn't be the first time he's done it, Jax. You know that."

Did he ever. He knew it better than anyone. He knew Trevor Hawkins was hurting from the loss of his friend years earlier, but Ralph's death had been Jax's responsibility. It was he who made the call to send HERO Force in, and Ralph's blood was on Jax's hands.

He wasn't about to make the same mistake again. Besides, his hands were tied. There was a reason he couldn't go after Steele. A reason he wasn't permitted to share.

Jax braced himself on the table. "Of course I know it. I also know the risk involved in sending a team up that mountain. Steele's resources are too great for one squad to take him down."

"So send two squads."

Jax slammed down a folder. "I can't justify that from this report, Hawk, and you damn well know it."

Hawk shook his head, his face reddening. "Two years we've been waiting for this, and you're just going to let it go?"

"It's my call." He turned to leave the conference room, but Hawk's voice stopped him cold.

"Then you're a coward."

Jax pivoted on his heel, taking deliberate steps back to Trevor Hawkins. They were friends. Brothers in arms. Had been through more together than most men would go through in a lifetime. But Jax was the leader of HERO Force, and Hawk had just crossed the one line Jax couldn't allow him to cross. "You just started your vacation two days early, Hawkins. Without pay."

Hawk said nothing, his eyes piercing Jax's across the room.

"When you come back to this team," said Jax, "you'd better remember who is where in the pecking order, or you won't be on this squad at all."

Yep. He should have seen it coming a mile away. Jax passed a woman in a formfitting business suit without making eye contact, then turned down another corridor. Several people walked toward him, and he nodded in greeting, his expression discouraging conversation.

A hundred yards down, he opened the door to a conference room and clenched his jaw as he took in the men at the table. This was the Alpha Squadron of HERO Force, a hand-picked team of ex-military and alphabet agency front men with the knowledge and experience to take on whatever might come their way.

He ought to know. He was the one who picked them.

"Gentlemen, I trust you all enjoyed your vacation."

Cowboy leaned on the back two legs of his chair,

holding the table for balance. "I was about to marry a Mexican princess when you called us back here."

Logan grinned, lacing his hands behind his head of wavy brown hair. "Finally found true love, eh, Cowboy?"

Cowboy touched the brim of his hat and winked. "Shit, Logan. I didn't say nothing about love."

Matteo crossed his arms. "Where's Hawk?"

"He's the reason I called you all back here," said Jax. "Hawk is on Warsaw Mountain."

"Ah, fuck." Cowboy leaned forward, slamming his chair to the floor with a loud thud.

"His cell phone was last pinpointed just over eleven miles from Steele's compound, but it doesn't seem to be currently transmitting," said Logan. "That means one of several things. It was destroyed or the battery was taken out in the hopes we wouldn't track him, or that cell communications in that area have been affected by the blizzard and subsequent, ongoing ice storm. The utilities are aware of several downed towers in that general vicinity."

"He wouldn't wait until he got there to take the battery out, if it was detection he was worried about," said Cowboy.

Jax shook his head. "Doesn't make a damn bit of difference why the signal stopped. It tells us he's there, or was there. It doesn't take a rocket scientist to figure out why. Likewise, there's no decision to be made about whether or not we go in after him. The only thing that's undecided is what our course of action should be. Stop him—if it's not too late to do that—or assist in his efforts to take down Steele."

Jax looked pointedly at Logan. "How strong is the intel you have right now?"

"Very strong." Logan opened his laptop. "We know for sure a shipment of girls arrived at his compound on the eighteenth."

"That was days ago," said Jax. "Steele wouldn't hold on to them a minute longer than necessary."

"True, but the road has been closed since the morning of the nineteenth." Logan raised his eyebrows. "There's a good chance those women are still there."

Matteo leaned back in his chair. "Steele could have heard the weather report and got them off the mountain before the road closed. Then we have no probable cause, and any action on Steele appears unjustified."

"Hawk is one of our own," said Jax. "But this mission isn't like our usual assignments. If this one goes bad, any or all of us might be brought up on charges of murder. I want each of you to think hard about this, but I want an answer right now. I'm going after Hawk. Are you coming with me?"

Cowboy raised his hand. "I'm in."

"I'm coming, too," said Logan, closing his laptop.

All eyes moved to Matteo.

"What do you say, Red?" asked Cowboy.

"I don't know him very well," said Matteo. He shrugged. "But I like to think a man you're all willing to die for must be someone I should defend."

Cowboy cracked a smile. "You could just say yeah, dude."

Jax wasn't amused. "Red, prepare the chopper. Cowboy, you pack. We leave at thirteen hundred hours."

The men stood up in unison and pushed in their chairs.

"It's high time someone went after that son of a bitch," said Jax.

CHAPTER 21

"D O YOU WANT to talk about it?" Trevor asked.

Olivia washed a pan in the sink, her back ramrod straight. They'd eaten in silence after she not-so-subtly told him to stop talking.

"There's nothing to talk about," she said. "I have no idea why I passed out. It's probably from the concussion."

"Livy, you were clearly upset about the heat exchanger."

"I was not upset, and stop calling me Livy. The furnace has nothing to do with me. This whole place has nothing to do with me."

The lady doth protest too much.

She knew he wasn't buying it for a minute.

"Besides, I don't want to talk about this," she said with a wave. "I thought we agreed not to talk about this." She dropped the pot onto a pile of other pots with a loud clang.

"You commanded me not to talk about it, actually," he said.

"This is ridiculous. Are you always such a child?"

His jaw dropped. "You're calling me a child?"

She turned around and put her hand on her hip. "Yes, I am."

God, she was gorgeous, with her hair falling this way and that from its rubber band, and the pissed-off flush of her skin. He was getting hard just looking at her, and he had no right to look at her like that at all.

"Fine," he said. "I won't say anything else about it tonight."

"Good."

He stared at her, unable to tear his eyes away. He wanted to kiss her again, to feel her defenses fall away as she responded to his touch. And she would respond to him. He was sure of it.

His hand twitched. He knew his desire was painted on his face, much like the high color in her cheeks suggested her own. If she so much as batted an eyelash, he'd be all over her.

She looked at the floor, breaking their connection, and he cleared his throat. "I'm going to go take a bath." His knee could use a good cold soak, which might help with his more pressing problem, as well.

He made his way into the bathroom, his mask of

nonchalance falling away. He eased the zipper of his jeans down and shucked them off, sitting on the cold edge of the tub and ignoring his hard-on. His knee was throbbing as much as his cock. How much damage had he done to it, pushing it when he knew he was injured?

He turned on the cold water, letting it run clear before filling the tub. He wished he had some ice to ease the swelling of his knee, but the cold water would have to do. He got in and leaned back against the icy enamel, his mind still full of Olivia's flushed face as she argued with him in the kitchen.

Man, she was beautiful, and somewhere out there was a man who knew it even better than he did. One lucky son of a bitch who'd asked her to marry him and she'd said yes, only now it was as if that had never happened, like the universe was offering her some perfect life or what was behind door number two—an embittered Navy SEAL who lived only to avenge his teammate's death.

Soon it would be time for them to sleep, and he already knew those blankets weren't enough to keep them both warm on separate couches, no matter who she was engaged to. He remembered what she felt like in his arms, so soft and curvy in all the right places, and his balls clenched with need despite the cold water.

There was a knock at the door. "I brought you some hot water," Olivia said as the door opened. "I thought you must be cold in here without…" She froze when her eyes reached his body, naked for her to see. "Oh, geez."

"Do the men you know bathe with their clothes on?"

Her cheeks were bright red. "You could have pulled the curtain when I came in."

"You didn't really give me the chance."

She pulled the curtain closed. "I'm sorry."

"I don't mind."

She was quiet for a moment. "What are we doing, Trevor?"

Torturing each other.

Dancing around each other and their growing attraction. Denying each other the one thing they wanted, and pretending it wasn't there.

"Nothing, unfortunately," he said.

She hit the shower curtain. "You know what I mean."

"Yes, I do."

She sighed. "Move your feet. I don't want to burn you." She dumped the water in, the most delicious warmth spreading through the tub, and he moaned with pleasure.

"You could join me," he said, his voice husky.

He could see her hand trail down the curtain, feel it as if it were touching his skin, then she turned and left the room, closing the door behind her.

So much for getting rid of his hard-on.

His hand closed around his shaft and he squeezed his cock tightly, then stroked it up and down. What would she feel like, her wet heat surrounding him?

A hell of a lot better than this, loser.

He sat up abruptly and splashed water on his face, then cleaned his body with punishing strokes. She had him acting like a horny teenager, and he wasn't enjoying the transition back in time. He hoisted himself up and out of the tub, pulled a towel around his waist and limped to the bedroom to get dressed.

When he made his way back to the living room, he froze. She was sleeping on one sofa, and the other had been made up for him. His disappointment was acute. He moved closer, all but certain she was pretending, but her breathing was deep and she really appeared to be sleeping.

He couldn't help but smile when he realized she was wearing several layers of clothing, including a trench coat.

Maybe it was for the best.

He tugged on a pair of boots and put on a coat, then grabbed his knife and headed out the door to do one last patrol before sleeping. The moon was shining brightly behind light cloud cover, enabling him to see quite well as he made his way around the property.

Back inside, he sat on the couch she'd readied for him, staring at her sleeping form. She had so many layers on, while he wore only a pair of sweat pants from the drawer. Of course, he knew he had no reason to be cold when Olivia was here, separate beds be damned.

He stood and moved to her, climbing over her legs and squeezing between her back and the sofa cushions, then spread his blanket over them both and tucked his arm around her middle possessively.

He could tell the moment she woke up, her lax muscles tightening with apprehension, but she didn't speak for several minutes.

"Is there something wrong with your bed?" she asked.

"You aren't in it."

The rhythm of her breathing quickened beneath his arm.

Olivia's arm snaked out from under the covers and she laced her fingers with his, pulling his arm more tightly around her as she shifted and placing her bottom snugly against him, driving him wild.

His face was in her hair and he nuzzled her neck before he could stop himself, his lips gently grazing her shoulder. She moaned, and he pulled her tightly to him.

"I'm sorry I made you angry," he whispered.

"Me, too."

He could make love to her just like that, let his hand that was already pressed against her chest wander to her breast, strip her of all those ridiculous clothes like he was unwrapping a present. Already she was pressing against his erection, her gentle motion a clear invitation.

Or was it? Did she know what she was doing to him?

He kissed her warm neck, the soft skin there that smelled so much like her, and she turned back to meet his kisses.

There it was, the quick and heavy chemistry, one touch of their mouths together proving what he suspected since the first time his eyes met hers. They would be good together. Perfectly matched to drive the other one crazy.

Any second now, she was going to stop him, tell him what a jerk he was for doing this to her, but he could tell she wanted him just as badly. He settled on top of her body. "Tell me we can't do this," he said. "Tell me you want me to stop."

He moved to the tie on her trench coat. She covered his hand with hers.

His voice was strained. "You're not going to let me undress you?" he asked, though he already knew the answer.

"I can't."

He hung his head and she wove her fingers through his hair, the edges of her fingernails touching his scalp. She kissed his forehead.

"You're killing me, Olivia." Reaching down, he circled her ankle and slowly pulled it up to his shoulder, feeling for any resistance and finding none. When she was open to him, he pressed himself against her, lust and frustration mingling into one tantalizing cocktail.

She squirmed beneath him.

"Feel me against you," he said. "Do you know how much I want you?"

"Yes, but we have to stop." She brought her leg back down, not meeting his eyes. "I'm sorry," she whispered. "I thought we could just kiss and be next to each other. I thought it might be enough."

"Enough?" He took hold of her jaw and tilted her chin up until her eyes met his. "I want to be inside you," he said. "I want to feel your body tighten around me when I make you come. I want to thrust inside you so hard I explode, and I want to hear your breathing settle in my ear and know that I did that to you." Her eyes were wide and her breath came quickly. He shook his head. "Nothing else will ever be enough."

He shifted his weight off of her, rolling her body so he was spooning her backside, and covered them with the blankets.

"What are you doing?" she asked.

"It's too cold for us to sleep on separate beds." He did his best to sound like it was no big deal, even though his body was screaming it was impossible. He was a Navy SEAL, for God's sake. He'd slept in more difficult situations than this. "You can relax, Livy. I'm not going to make another move on you tonight."

"You expect me to just go to sleep, with… *that*?"

He knew she was referring to his cock against her backside. "Not a lot I can do about that right now. Just do me a favor and try to control yourself. And whatever you do, don't wiggle your butt."

CHAPTER 22

OLIVIA LAID IN the circle of Trevor's arms, her traitorous body refusing to sleep. What had possessed her to kiss him when he nuzzled her neck?

Lust.

Oh, she lusted after him, all right. She wanted that man as much as he wanted her, but she was torn and feeling utterly responsible for her as-of-yet-unmemorable fiancé.

What if she did remember him, and suddenly regretted all of her actions with Trevor? It seemed the most likely scenario, so keeping Trevor at bay made sense. But fifteen minutes after his breathing became deeper and more rhythmic, she could still feel the pressure of his boner on her bottom, and was still forcing her pelvis to be still when she desperately wanted to press back against him.

She sighed heavily.

What would this night have been like if she'd welcomed his advances? They would have made love, that was for sure. It seemed all that man had to do was look at her and she skipped through fourteen kinds of foreplay in one hot second.

She didn't want to behave and "do the right thing" where Trevor was concerned, and she wasn't sure if that made her a petulant child or a grown-up woman who'd been given a once-in-a-lifetime opportunity. A chance to experience another man, at a time when that chance should have been far behind her.

Trevor stirred in his sleep, his arm tightening around her middle. She slipped her hand over his. Even his hands showed the strength of his body, each finger heavily muscled and devoid of any fat. He was the epitome of the strong male physique, so she shouldn't be surprised by her reaction to him. This was nature and sexual attraction at their best.

She sighed dramatically.

She was *never* going to get any sleep.

CHAPTER 23

OLIVIA HAD BEEN walking around on eggshells all day. Trevor was in a foul mood, and to make matters worse, the weather seemed to be deteriorating instead of getting better.

They'd grown accustomed to the snow and freezing rain, but the wind had really picked up speed, making it nearly impossible to be outdoors at all. Of course, that hadn't stopped Trevor from patrolling the area twice already.

"We could play a game," she suggested.

"I have things I have to do."

"Yes, but you can't get outside to do them, so maybe you should find something to do besides pace the living room and sulk."

He'd slept like a baby, but she'd lain awake all night, certain she'd made the wrong decision. What was the point of being faithful to a man you couldn't remember, when you were desperate for the one right in front of you?

"Don't worry. I'm not going to touch you," he said.

"That's not fair."

"I wasn't necessarily going for fair." He walked to the front window, then circled back to the kitchen. "I'm going stir-crazy in here."

She frowned.

"No offense," he added. "I didn't come to Warsaw Mountain to sit around."

"Tell me about your friend."

"Excuse me?" he asked.

"Your friend. The one you were on your way to visit."

He plopped down in a chair. "I wasn't on my way to see a friend."

"But you said…"

"I lied." He shrugged. "I'm sorry. I didn't know you very well at the time."

She swallowed. Why did it matter if he was seeing someone? She certainly was. Or so it would seem, anyway. She worked to smooth out the jealous lines she knew were affecting her expression. "A woman?"

His eyes shot to hers. "No. There is no woman."

She wrenched her eyes away. "Oh."

"I had this friend, Ralph," he said. "We were on the Teams together—Navy SEALs—right from

BUD/S training, the very beginning."

"What happened to him?"

"He was murdered two years ago, right on this mountain."

She gasped. "Do you know who killed him?"

"Yes. I'm just waiting for the weather to break before I make my move."

The steely look in his eye was beginning to make her uncomfortable. "And then what? Are you going to call the police?"

"Not exactly." He stood up and walked to the kitchen, peering out the window. "Just out of curiosity, what game did you want to play?"

She wondered what "not exactly" meant but wasn't sure she wanted to ask. From the look in his eyes, Trevor was going to extract his own kind of justice from Ralph's killer. "How about checkers?"

"We don't have any checkers."

"We could make some."

He eyed her grumpily.

"I mean, I could make some," she said. She stood up. "Why don't I do that."

Fifteen minutes later, they were playing checkers made with two different pasta shapes and a board drawn on a piece of paper. Two hours later, she was winning, three games to two, and Trevor was actually smiling.

"I'm going to have a drink," he announced.

"Would you like one?" He took the unlabeled bottle down from the mantel. "I have no idea what this is."

"That sounds perfect."

He poured them each a glass and sat back down. "Do we have to play more checkers?" he asked.

"I thought you were enjoying yourself."

"I was enjoying you trying to cheer me up." He took a swig of his drink. "You're cute."

She tentatively sipped the liquor and was pleased with its cinnamon flavor, then let it burn its way down her throat. "It was hell on earth, that's what it was."

"Oh, come on. I wasn't that bad."

She laughed out loud. "I'd rather be trapped in a bus station in Cheboygan at three in the morning than play checkers with you in a bad mood again."

"I'm sorry, Livy, for the way I acted last night."

"It's okay."

"No, it's not. If you don't want to be with me, I should respect that and back off, not pressure you."

She could feel her cheeks getting hot as she remembered the press of his cock against her.

"Anyway, it won't happen again."

"I was giving you mixed signals. I was the one who wasn't being fair."

"You're allowed to change your mind."

"Well," she said, not believing she was going to say this, even as the words formed on her tongue, "I changed it again after you fell asleep. I swear, I was up all night."

His eyes darkened and she felt the tension between them tighten and pull.

"My turn to pick the entertainment," he said, standing and walking toward her. For a moment, she thought he was heading toward her and his "entertainment" involved little more than himself, but he kept walking and left the room, returning with the radio. "Do you like to dance?" he asked.

It was a challenge.

Her stomach fluttered with the idea of being so close to him again. All day she'd been thinking about him, about the feel of him against her and the words he'd said about only sex being enough. "Sure I do." She took a bigger sip of her drink and stood, just as he settled on a station with a slow song playing.

He held out a hand and she put hers in it, letting him lead her into the circle of his arms.

I want to be inside you.

The memory of his earlier words rang in her head. He grazed her skin with his fingers, and goose bumps trailed along her arms. His hand settled on the small of her back, warm and wide and strong.

I want to feel your body tighten around me when I make you come.

She was getting excited already, and she let her head rest on his shoulder. How easily she could turn her head and kiss his skin, feel it beneath her lips and lick it with her tongue.

I want to thrust inside of you so hard I explode.

They were moving to the music, their footsteps easily falling into synch, and she realized she should have expected no less from this man. If there was a man out there somewhere who fit with her better, she couldn't imagine who he was.

Then I want to hear your breathing settle in my ear and know that I did that to you.

She ran her hands along the top of his back, loving how he moaned softly beneath her ear.

He stroked her back, her arms, down the sides of her breasts. "I can't keep myself from touching you," he said. "I know I shouldn't do it, and I don't want you to regret anything we do together, but my hands seem to think they belong on your skin, and you feel so damn good."

She turned her mouth to his neck and kissed him as she'd wanted to do. His skin was salty on her tongue. "It's like we're in a bubble," she said. "Nothing and no one exists outside of this cabin." She met his eyes, then looked at his lips, so curvy and full. Lips made for loving. "For me, there isn't any 'before' and there isn't any 'after.' So when you say you don't want me to be sorry, I can't even imagine what that looks like."

She touched his chest. "We're in this crazy situation, and the only thing I want right now is you. Just tell me you wouldn't lie to me. Tell me you'd never keep a secret from me, and let's be together. I want to make love to you tonight, Trevor."

He held her face in his hands and sighed. "There's just one more thing."

CHAPTER 24

O LIVIA STARED AT the garment bag on the back of the door as if it were radioactive. Trevor had stood in the doorway for what seemed like hours, the space between them heavy and solid, before finally placing the hanger onto the hook and quietly closing the bedroom door.

This made everything real.

She raised the back of her hand to her lips, choking back a sob. Trevor. She let her eyes close, giving herself up to the grief that washed over her. They'd been living in a fantasy world, one where she had only the clothes on her back and the problems of a newborn babe, a magical place where this man had become the center of her universe, the one and only person she ever wanted to be with, the man who felt like home to the woman who couldn't remember if she had one.

She turned and walked to the window, hugging herself tightly. Outside, the last rays of sunlight danced on ice-covered branches, the wind making the trees tremble and shake. This should be the night they'd make love, when she would open her body to Trevor as she had already opened her heart. An image of his golden-brown eyes appeared in her mind, and she grimaced as she realized all she had lost.

Trevor. A man strong enough for her to lean on and then some. Most important, she trusted him. There was a man who would never betray her, never let her down. His conscience wouldn't allow it.

Had someone let her down before? Was there a man in her past who made her so desperate for the security she found with Trevor?

If she turned back now, she wouldn't be able to have him. To feel his skin, sweaty and hot from wanting her, loving her, his body pressed against her own desperate flesh. Frustration had her clutching her hands into fists.

He didn't have to tell her about the dress. About any of it. He could have kept his mouth shut and she would have fallen to her knees in front of him. But he had told her, bringing her the dress like the last dollar in the pocket of a pauper, and as she stood in front of the window, cold radiating from its panes, she hated him for his honesty, for that damn sense of honor that required him to set the record straight before she yanked and ripped the clothes from his body.

"Son of a bitch," she muttered, lightly banging her head against the wooden window grill. He was in the next room mere steps from where she stood, but it might as well have been a football field from her for all she was able to do about it.

She didn't know how long she stood there. Long enough for the cross of the grill to sink into her forehead and her anger to slowly drain into the floor. Turning around, she took in the garment bag, needing to see the dress inside. To see if it fit, if the style suited her, if she could possibly be the same woman who had picked it out and smiled and twirled, imagining her life with some ghost of a man long since forgotten. To see if she still wanted to be that woman, or to become someone else.

Crossing the room with harried steps, she ripped down the zipper and frowned.

The tiniest white beads and miniature iridescent sequins shined back at her. Olivia brought a tentative hand up to touch the fabric, impressed with its detail and workmanship. Whoever she was, she must have money, because a dress like this surely didn't come cheap.

Pushing the plastic open and down, she revealed the gown in its entirety, releasing a breath as she dropped her shoulders.

It was exquisite, unlike anything she'd seen before.

She removed her sweater and pulled the hem of her T-shirt over her head. This dress was a relic from another time and place when she knew who she was and what she wanted. It seemed impossible that it would fit, as if the woman she'd become over these last few days with Trevor could have changed her very shape and form.

As she slid her jeans down over her panties, she was struck by her hopes of making love to Trevor and how incredibly different this day had turned out. Twisting to see herself in the dresser mirror, she took in her bare lace brassiere and low-hanging bikini. This outfit was for him. All of this for Trevor. She stared at her own glassy expression, then her eyes closed and her hand dipped over her mound, cupping herself there, imagining her fingers belonged to the man outside that door.

All of this was for you.

A wave of dizziness had her inhaling quickly. The dress. She had to put on the dress and this awful spell would be broken. If the truth in her heart could only be proven, she would be free like the wrong woman trying on Cinderella's slipper. Olivia gently lifted the straps from the hanger and dressed without looking at herself again. When she managed to maneuver the skinny zipper all the way up her back, she opened her eyes and her mouth dropped open.

Not only did the dress fit her perfectly, she looked incredible. The fabric seemed to hug her breasts, displaying them to graceful advantage, as the cut of the entire bodice seemed to drape her in femininity. Reaching down, she picked up the swirling skirt, the perfect balance of traditional fullness and refined lines.

This was her wedding dress. There could be no doubt about it. Her very real dress that she'd picked out for her very real wedding to a very real man she must love.

She whipped around, staring accusingly out that same frosty window, anger rushing in where emptiness had been. She wanted to kick out the panes, smash the wood grill with her bare hands, tear this cute little cabin to shreds. It wasn't fair, wasn't right, anything she was feeling. This night was supposed to belong to her and Trevor, but instead that had been ripped from her hands and this fucking dress left in its place.

There was a knock at the door. "Olivia?"

She was breathing heavily and awareness prickled down her spine. What would she give if she could rewind the clock, tell him she didn't want to see whatever it was he wanted to show her? She could have slipped her hands beneath his clothing, touching him intimately until he gave her everything she knew would make them both happy.

"Yes?"

He was quiet so long she wondered if she heard her. She reached up and touched the wooden door. He was hurting, too. He wanted her, too. Shared her feelings.

She closed her eyes and sighed. Heaven help her, she still wanted to make love to him.

Her eyes opened wide. Could she do that? Just make love to Trevor as if nothing else mattered, even the man she was engaged to marry? She was bound to him by a promise she couldn't remember making.

That man is a stranger to me.

How could you betray someone you didn't even know?

Her heart began to race as the possibilities crystalized. "This is crazy," she whispered. It was one thing to make love to Trevor when she had no knowledge of her life, but she was standing here staring at herself in her wedding dress, knowing she was promised to another man as she considered loving this one anyway.

A warm flush spread up her chest to her neck and cheeks.

Trevor's voice was tight and gravelly. "I should have given you the dress when I found it. I don't know why I didn't."

She opened the door, watching as his chin lifted and his eyes raked over every inch of her body, finally colliding with her own. She could feel the pain in his stare, the heat, and knew what the sight of her was doing to him. Looking at him was doing the exact same thing to her.

The knowledge made her bold. "I know why you didn't tell me." She took a deep breath. This was right.

No matter what happened later, outside these walls and away from here, making love to this man could only ever be right. "Because the electricity between us is enough to light up every house on this mountainside, and you didn't want to let that go any more than I do."

His eyes seemed to sparkle at the mention of the lust that was in full bloom. He shook his head slightly. "It was wrong."

Their time together was slipping away, reality encroaching on her dreams. If she didn't do something quickly, Trevor Hawkins would be nothing but a memory, and everything that had been lost to her would rise up to cover her head like water.

But he was an honorable man, and what she wanted from him was anything but honorable. Steeling herself against his rejection, she stepped toward him, lightly resting her fingers on his shoulder. "I still want to make love to you, Trevor."

He stared at her, suspended, his eyes locked with hers and dilating.

"If you'll have me," she whispered. The first inkling of fear settled into her stomach. Oh God, he was going to turn her down. She could feel it. She slipped her hand down his arm. "Please," she begged.

A look of raw hunger overtook his features, and he kissed her. She welcomed his arms as he wrapped them around her possessively. She needed to feel her skin against his, her naked chest desperate to rub against his pecs and chest hair.

"Get me out of this dress," she said against his mouth.

He pulled back just enough to meet her stare with a harsh look of his own. "No," he growled. "Leave the dress on."

CHAPTER 25

TREVOR WAS OVERCOME with the need to possess her. Telling her about the ring and dress had been the most difficult things he'd ever done, yet here she was, choosing to share herself with him even after she learned the truth.

He grabbed her hips and pressed against layers of fabric, finding the softness between her legs and grinding his hardening cock against her there.

She let out a gasp.

In his hands he held fistfuls of the wedding dress she'd bought to marry another man, and he had a desperate need to claim her as his own. To prove her clothing held no power to keep them apart, that what they shared was stronger than fancy beads and lace or any promises that came before this moment.

He lifted his head and saw the arousal on her

flushed face, then kissed down the side of her neck to her bodice, tracing its edge with his tongue.

Olivia murmured and reached down, arching her back as she pushed the fabric down to expose her lace-covered breasts. The sight of her dark nipples inside the gossamer bra made him growl with need. He had to taste her, had to feel her against his tongue, press his lips into the soft flesh of her breast. He took her into his mouth, suckling her through the garment. She keened loudly, her hips bucking wildly against him.

He breathed against her there. "You're so beautiful."

She pushed the cups of her bra all the way down, exposing the nipple, wet and erect from his mouth. He took what she offered and latched firmly on to her skin, drawing her nipple deep into his mouth and sucking out a drop of her sweetness. She went wild.

He could feel his cock straining against his shorts, so anxious was he to be inside her. Swooping down with one arm, he picked her up from behind her knees and carried her to the bed, the fullness of her skirt nearly reaching his face. She hit the bed with a bounce and pulled him down on top of her.

"I need you inside me," she said breathlessly.

Leaning away from her, he found the hem of her dress and began lifting the layers up over her waist until he bared her legs and tiny underwear. He could barely see her face, only her smooth, shapely legs and the junction that waited for him to enter, surrounded by layers and layers of tulle.

He ran his hands up her legs until he rested between them. He inhaled the scent of sex and knew he'd never smelled anything more arousing. He unfastened his belt and unzipped his fly, instantly growing even bigger, more eager, more excited.

"Roll over," he commanded, and she did.

He found the top of the zipper on her dress and slid it down, over the small of her back and the top of her ass. Then he peeled it off of her, freeing her body from the confines of the fabric, and sliding off her underwear.

He rolled her back over, glorying in the sight of her completely naked. He was going to be inside her, stroking her most sensitive flesh, and he knew he'd never wanted anyone more. He sunk his fingers into her soft curls and found her opening dripping with dew, just as he was.

Had a woman ever been so eager for his touch? So desperate to be as close to him as he was to her?

"God, you are so lovely," he said reverently. "And so ready for me." He gently teased her clitoris and let his finger slip lower. "So sweet and wet."

She thrust her hips forward, her sex pursuing his hand. "Please, Trevor!"

He slipped his fingers inside her and she bucked and moaned. He chuckled devilishly. "Is that what you want?"

"No." She met his stare. "I want you inside me. I want you to be inside me when I come."

The thought of her convulsing around his shaft overwhelmed him. Moving quickly, he shucked off his pants and briefs and settled himself between her legs, loving the way she opened to him. He kissed her, teasing her mouth with his tongue, and when she responded, he pressed inside her in one long thrust.

She yelped, her body going rigid.

"Did I hurt you?"

She shook her head. "No. Just give me a second."

He felt her relax around him and clench him tightly, then relax again as she drew him in even deeper than before. The feeling was sweet torture, and he began to move inside her.

Her eyes flew open. "Don't move," she said, sliding up and down his cock in one tantalizing movement.

He began to pant. "You're killing me."

She smiled from half her mouth. "I'm just getting warmed up." She arched her back, then pressed her hips forward, taking his whole length. "Now."

She didn't have to tell him twice. Trevor buried his face in her neck and began to move. Each thrust was better than the last, the pressure inside him building with every stroke. It didn't matter who she was engaged to, he was going to explode.

He pulled out. "Get on your knees," he commanded, and watched as she did as she was told, turning her ass toward him and arching her back so that its roundness and the crease between her swollen sex stood out.

He could have been a lion mounting his mate, so primal was his need to have her. He entered her roughly and she called out loud. He reached around her torso and grabbed a breast in each hand, squeezing her hard while he pumped into her from behind. "I don't care what you remember. You'll always belong to me."

The sound she was making changed as her body clenched him tightly and she came fiercely around him, the spasms of her orgasm bringing on his own, bright and blinding. He came deep into her sweetness, retreating and thrusting again.

They stayed like that, fitted together, her body sucking at him as aftershocks rippled through her. There was just the sound of their breathing and the soft sounds of pleasure as they slowly came back to earth.

Trevor lifted himself off her back and took in the sight of his body still nestled in hers. This was right. Every touch, every movement, every sensation they shared. This was right, no matter who was waiting for her outside of this cabin.

"Trevor," she said on a moan.

Olivia rested her elbows on the mattress and her

ass tilted upward. In the faint light of the room, he caught the shadow of something down low on her left cheek.

A tattoo.

He narrowed his eyes and froze.

Brooke.

Brooke Barrons. The movie star. Olivia was so plain, so real, so naturally pretty, he never associated her with the overdone starlet. But now the resemblance was both obvious and startling. Everyone who stood in the checkout line at the grocery store knew about Brooke Barrons' engagement. She'd said several times on national television that she would not reveal the identity of her fiancé until the wedding was complete.

He traced the outline of the tattoo with his finger. "Livy?"

"Hmm?"

"You're not going to believe this, but I think you're a movie star."

CHAPTER 26

L OGAN O'MALLEY WIPED snow from the bent steel frame of Trevor's truck and frowned.

"Well?" asked Jax.

"Striations on the steel indicate explosives were detonated inside the vehicle."

"After the crash or causing the crash?"

"There's no way to tell for sure. C-4 is relatively stable, but you can get it to detonate if you try hard enough. Depending on the car accident, it might have ignited."

Cowboy whistled from the other side of the vehicle. "Looks like Hawk was packing more than C-4. I've got enough munitions over here to poke holes through half of Texas."

Jax turned slowly in a circle, his eyes taking in the frozen landscape, interrupted only by the HERO

Force chopper still idling in the distance. He didn't like being so damned obvious and visible this close to Steele's territory, but the storm had limited their options.

These cars had clearly fallen from farther up the mountain, though where exactly was far less clear. Hawk had been on his way up Warsaw Mountain when this accident had sent his truck and the other car back down into this ravine.

But where the hell was Hawk? Acid churned in Jax's stomach, burning in the spot where he'd once had an ulcer. When they got to the last known coordinates transmitted from his cell phone, they didn't even see the cars. They'd had to dig through two feet of snow just to uncover the wreckage, and another three feet with their hearts in their throats as they worked to uncover their friend.

Jax had a lot of time to think while they dug through that snow. Thoughts of his history with Hawk, their time on the Teams together, how instrumental Hawk had been in starting HERO Force.

How important Hawk had been in his own life, more like a brother than a friend.

Jax knew what Ralph's death had done to Hawk, and he knew the damage he himself had done by refusing to avenge Ralph's death. He'd made a phone call today before they left headquarters. A phone call that made him free to go after Steele as he hadn't been free to before. The irony was almost too much to bear. They were digging for Hawk's dead body, and Jax could finally give the go-ahead to kill Steele.

But Hawk wasn't there.

Thank God. Jax could have wept, he was so relieved. He couldn't stand the blood of another HERO Force member on his hands, as Ralph's was. That was a stain Jax could never wash off.

And poor Jessa…

He slammed the door on his thoughts. There was a time and place to think about Ralph and all that had transpired, and it usually involved Jax being alone in the dark with a bottle of whiskey.

Matteo climbed out of the chopper with a laptop in his hands and made his way to Jax. "Satellite imagery of Warsaw Mountain taken last winter. You can see Steele's compound at the top, just over eleven miles from here, but I count seven other buildings on this side of the mountain, the closest of which is only one-point-two miles north-northeast from here." He handed the papers to Jax.

"So that's the closest shelter, but what are the chances he would have found that one?"

"The other buildings are each more than ten miles from this location, sir."

Cowboy approached, his hands on his hips as he waited. "There's blood in the truck. Enough to indicate an injury, though not necessarily anything severe.

There are marks on the dashboard where the left leg would have been, and several drops on the carpet and the door."

"So he was hurt," says Jax. "What about the other car?"

"No blood, no obvious signs of injury prior to the explosion and impact."

"Someone must have been driving it." Jax furrowed his brow. "Or maybe it was abandoned on the road due to the storm."

Cowboy nodded. "Possible."

Jax looked up the mountain again, his eyes focusing on the first ledge above their current location, some hundred feet higher than they stood. "A lot of things are possible. Let's focus on probable for a minute." He pointed to the ledge. "That's probably our accident scene. How far is it from there to that cabin you were showing me?"

Matteo nodded. "Just over a mile. A straight shot up the road."

"We go there first," said Jax. "If we don't find him, we go to the next most likely place he could be."

"My money says he's at the top of the mountain," said Cowboy. "If Hawk had a day's breath in him, he'd have gone on up there and done what he came here to do."

Jax glared at him. "Eleven miles is too far to go on foot in these conditions, especially if he's injured."

Cowboy moved to walk past him. "I don't know. Where I come from, y'all can make a pig fly if you want to badly enough."

CHAPTER 27

OLIVIA WOKE TO the sunlight warming her eyelids and stretched languidly on the bed, her foot running into Trevor's. She smiled, curling up to his side and smelling the spicy scent of his body—a body she'd gotten to know well over the last twelve hours.

Now that the fire was out, there was no reason to forsake the comfort of the bed and the space it offered in favor of the couch in the living room, and she was enjoying the freedom to stretch out nearly as much as she was enjoying being too close to Trevor's body.

They'd made love time after time through the night, dozing in each other's arms and taking turns waking to the other's passion.

Trevor's arm tightened around her and she sighed. Sex with him was so much better than sex with Marco. Her eyes popped open.

Marco.

Her heart began to race, a cold sweat breaking out on her palms. Her mind tentatively picked up her memories of Marco and flipped through them with shaking fingers. She could remember his face, his hands, his naked body.

His penis.

Trevor had a cock, but Marco had a penis. She'd never found Marco's penis interesting or attractive, but she'd taken Trevor's cock in her mouth and sucked him deep into her throat like the most luscious candy.

She looked at her ring finger, so empty without the large engagement ring she'd finally gotten used to seeing there.

It was all coming back to her like waves flooding the beach, covering toys and chairs and towels while people ran for safety.

Marco, her benefactor. She and Marco got engaged after Ellie and Frank died. Just thinking about it whet her grief again, the shock of losing her best friend, Ellie, and her best friend's father to carbon monoxide poisoning in this cabin.

Their deaths had thrown her into a deep depression.

And now she knew they'd been murdered.

But by whom?

Marco had been so helpful, so understanding, knowing she didn't want to stay in the cabin she inherited and moving her in with him, never even hinting he was romantically interested until the day he proposed.

She'd said yes in a heartbeat. She'd needed him so much, desperately needed someone to lean on now that Ellie and Frank were gone.

Trevor moaned softly in his sleep.

She was afraid to move, scared even her breathing would wake him completely and force her to look him in the eye before she'd soaked up all that was happening. Her horror was screaming from her pores, and she knew without a doubt he would take one look at her and know something was terribly, terribly wrong.

She needed to remember. She needed to remember it all.

She had been a virgin, and she and Marco were going to wait to have sex until they got married, but she'd gotten scared. What if sex with him was unpleasant, and she didn't discover it until it was too late? He was older than her, and she worried the age difference would be too much.

So she'd forced the issue, coming into his bedroom that first night in her frilly pink gown and lying beside him in clear invitation. The first time had been painful, Marco's long, skinny dick poking in and out of her while he grunted, but over the next few months he proved himself a competent lover, or so she'd believed.

Now she knew she'd never really been turned on,

never been truly wet or swollen with desire for a man. The pleasant feelings Marco had brought out in her body had more in common with a back rub than they had with the crazed and desperate desire that was summoned and fulfilled by Trevor.

She closed her eyes, remembering how she stared at the calendar in total panic, counting down the days until her marriage to Marco. She was booked on Saturday Night Live for publicity, to lead everyone on about who she might be marrying, each appearance making her less able to breathe than the last, and Marco more gleeful.

SNL marked the two-week point. Two weeks until the wedding.

She'd felt like she was going to die.

But why? What had happened to make her change her mind?

Trevor kissed the top of her head and she squeezed her eyes shut.

"Good morning, sleepyhead," he whispered, pulling her more tightly against him. He rubbed up her arms and over her back and buttocks, lightly scraping her with his nails. Then he was massaging her thighs, easing them apart and moving his leg between them.

Heaven help her, she still wanted this man. Even after everything she remembered, she didn't want him to stop. What did that say about her? Her entire world had just exploded into chaos, and she was happily spreading her legs for just one more fuck before the sky fell down.

His head moved to her breast and he took her in his mouth, licking and sucking one nipple while he tended the other with his hand, and she couldn't help the way her head pushed back against the pillow. She didn't want this to stop, didn't want reality to intervene and force him away from her.

His knee came up, pressing against her most sensitive places, and she thrust her hips forward.

He kissed along her neck, his lower body lining up with hers, the head of his cock just touching the entrance to her body. Trevor thrust inside her and she called out, her body slightly sore and super sensitive, the mixture of pleasure and pain more arousing than she would have thought possible.

"Am I hurting you?" he asked.

"God, no."

He thrust into her harder than before and she called out again, their bodies perfectly synchronized.

The waves that had been flooding her memory faded into the background as her body took control, welcoming her lover into herself, and a fierce storm burst inside her. He thrust into her faster and faster until he came, too, his orgasm making him shudder and shout.

They collapsed onto the bed, their bodies still joined together.

She had to tell him.

If they were going to be honest with each other, she had to let him know she'd regained such an important part of her memory. Marco. The man she'd been planning to marry.

And what would become of them now? Could she possibly go on seeing Trevor while engaged to Marco, or would she have to choose one or the other?

Someone knocked harshly on the front door and their eyes met in surprise.

"Who could that be?" she asked.

Trevor hopped off the bed, pulling on his jeans and zipping them over his naked body. "Stay here."

CHAPTER 28

H AWK HELD THE knife in his hand and peered out the window beside the door, beneath the cereal box he's used to patch the hole. Jax was on the porch, with Cowboy, Matteo, and Logan standing behind him. Cowboy bent his head toward the window and waved at Hawk as he would a toddler.

Two things occurred to Hawk at once. Logan had ratted him out, and it had finally stopped snowing.

Hawk opened the door and met Jax's stony stare. Hawk stepped back for them to enter. "Hello, Logan," he said pointedly.

Logan looked from Hawk to Jax and back. "I'm sorry, Hawk."

"No problem. It's always good to know who's got my six and who doesn't."

Jax turned his head sharply. "Don't you put this on

him. This is all you, Hawk. From the moment you heard the first intel on Steele, you were packing your bags, HERO Force and my orders be damned."

Trevor raised his chin. "I'm doing this for HERO Force. I'm doing this for Ralph. Do you remember Ralph, Jax? Tall guy, about six three…"

Jax pushed Trevor in the collarbone, making him take a stumbling step back. "How dare you imply I don't take care of my men?"

"Then why don't you act like it, huh? Why don't you go after that bastard yourself instead of chastising me for doing it?"

"Outside," commanded Jax. "We need to talk."

Olivia appeared in the hallway. "Uh, excuse me."

The men turned toward her in unison. Someone hummed appreciatively.

"This is Olivia Grayson," said Hawk. "We were in a car accident together."

Cowboy walked over and tipped his hat. "How you doin', ma'am? I'm Leo Wilson, but you can call me Cowboy." He winked.

She bit her lip. "Trevor, may I speak to you for a minute?"

Matteo raised his eyebrows and said quietly, "I think you're in trouble, *Trevor*."

Trevor put his hand on her shoulder. "Give us a minute."

"But I need to tell you something." She looked

upset, and he didn't blame her. The team could be overwhelming, and from her rosy cheeks and bed-tossed hair, it wasn't hard to imagine what they'd been doing. She must be embarrassed.

He touched her shoulder and ushering her back in the bedroom. "It won't take long, Livy."

"If you don't mind me saying, it's colder than a witch's tit in here," said Cowboy. "You got any wood for a fire?"

Trevor shoved his feet into the ski boots. "We can't be seen."

Jax held open the door and Hawk stepped outside, crossing his arms and squinting against the sunshine.

"How'd you find me?" Hawk asked.

"GPS in your phone."

"The explosion didn't knock that little fucker out?"

"It sends a ping every few minutes. We used your last known coordinates."

"If I knew you were coming, I'd have baked a cake."

Jax crossed to Hawk. "Is this a fucking joke to you?" he asked. "Dragging all of Alpha Squadron across the country after you were given a direct order not to pursue Steele?"

Hawk took a good look at his friend, his SEAL brother. They'd been through more together than most people could imagine. Fought for their country, for right over wrong and good versus evil. They'd gone through Ralph's death together. Then somehow, Jax had just disappeared. Let Hawk down. Dropped the most important ball he'd ever held in his hands. Steele.

Hawk shook his head. "You're the joke, Jax."

Jax punched him square in the belly. Trevor doubled over but came up swinging, catching Jax's cheek and nose with the solid uppercut they'd been begging for for years.

It felt good to hit Jax. It even felt good to be hit, knowing from this display that Jax hid some kind of emotion about Ralph down deep inside. It was Jax's apathy that had been so hard to bear. His canned answer about good tactical decisions and bad, month after month, while their friend rotted in the ground and Hawk ached.

The punches flew, with a random kick thrown in for good measure, until the men were bloodied, sweaty, and worn.

Jax spit out blood. "You're out of HERO Force, as of right now."

"Tell me why you did it," said Trevor. "Tell me what was so important to you that you sat back on your heels and let Steele get away with murdering Ralph."

"You think that's what I wanted? That I enjoyed letting that fucker walk this earth after what he did? Hell no! Homeland Security told me to back off. They were in the middle of an active investigation and if we interfered in any way, years of working to get Steele would be washed down the drain."

Trevor shook his head. "Why the hell didn't you tell me?"

"It was need-to-know, damn it. I couldn't tell you."

"And you don't think I needed to know? You didn't fucking trust me?"

"It wasn't my call. My hands were tied, Hawk. There wasn't a damn thing I could do without HERO Force getting blown out of the water, until now."

"What's changed?"

"When you went rogue and came out here to pursue Steel, I had to notify Homeland Security. I was told their investigation is on hold indefinitely."

"Why?"

Jax shook his head. "Don't know. Don't care." He met Trevor's stare. "Ralph's waited long enough for justice, don't you think?"

Hawk put his arms in the air. "Booyah! We're going to get that motherfucker!"

Jax shook his head. "You're staying here."

"*What?*"

"Insubordination. If I can't trust you off the field, I sure as hell can't trust you on it."

Hawk covered his mouth and squeezed his cheeks.

Jax was right, that was the worst part. Classic military methodology. Hawk's mind raced. "But you need me. I know how to stop Steele from taking the women away. I have access to a walkie-talkie that's connected to someone right in his compound, and I know the only entryway that isn't secured."

"Give me what you've got, Hawk."

Hawk stared at him, determined to win this battle of wills. "No way. You wouldn't be here if it wasn't for me. I'm the one who watched Ralph die; I'm the one who wouldn't let it go. I deserve to be there, damn it."

Jax cursed under his breath. "Fine, but it doesn't mean you've got your job back."

"Deal."

They went back inside.

"Leave the door open," said Cowboy. "It's warmer out there than it is in here." He cocked his head and looked at Hawk. "It's a miracle you two didn't freeze to death. How'd y'all keep warm, anyway?" A devilish grin spread across his face.

Matteo chuckled.

"Shut up, Cowboy," said Hawk.

Jax's voice rose above the others. "Tell me why you can't be seen. You're far enough from Steele's house you shouldn't have a problem."

"Steele's goons came around, looking for a runaway from his current shipment." He filled them in on the mysterious snowmobiler and the radio call.

"Good for the one who got away," said Matteo.

Trevor crossed his arms. "We have to save the rest of those girls."

Jax nodded. "Agreed. Tell us what you know about the compound, and we'll make our plan."

CHAPTER 29

OLIVIA HUDDLED AGAINST the cold, listening to the rise and fall of the men's voices down the hall. Trevor's *it won't take long* had turned into more than half an hour, time she'd spent worrying about his reaction to her memory returning.

Had he forgotten she was in here, waiting for him?

The arrival of his teammates brought out another side of Trevor she hadn't seen before, a side battered in testosterone and fried in adrenaline.

The bedroom door opened and she jumped.

"Sorry I took so long," said Trevor. "What's up?"

He came and sat on the bed beside her. The energy coming from him belied his casual pose, as if he could bolt into action at any moment.

She licked her lips. "I remembered something. Or someone."

His brows came together. "Who?"

"My fiancé."

He sat up straighter. "Oh."

"I thought you should know, now that we…we're lovers and everything."

"How do you feel about him?"

"I don't know. I'm feeling a lot of things, honestly."

"I see."

"No, Trevor, I don't think you do." She looked at her hands. "I don't remember everything yet, but I know I was running away from my own wedding. I wasn't going to marry him."

"You weren't?"

"No."

"I don't know why, but I almost think I was afraid of him."

"Did he abuse you?"

She shook her head. "I don't know. I wish I could explain… It's like trying to guess the final picture of a jigsaw puzzle when you only have a few of the pieces."

He took her hand in his. "You have time. You don't need to remember everything this moment."

Someone rapped three times on the bedroom door. "Wheels up in five minutes, Hawk."

Olivia looked to the door, then back at Trevor. "What's going on?"

"They're going to help me go after Ralph's killer."

She still didn't want to know exactly what he meant

by *go after*, but she smiled because she knew what their support meant to him. "That's great."

"I want you to come with us back to the chopper. You'll be safe there while we complete the mission."

She thought back to the panic and fear she'd experienced the last time he'd left her alone. "I thought you'd never ask."

CHAPTER 30

T HEY'D LEFT OLIVIA in the chopper and traveled up the mountain on three-man ATVs, each of them equipped with the night vision goggles and com system they'd need on the journey. This was the stuff HERO Force was good at—infiltrating enemy territory—and Hawk was grateful the mission that would have been trying as a solo operation now had the full capabilities of the team.

Nearly everything Trevor lost in the crash, HERO Force had brought with them to Warsaw Mountain. The chopper was loaded with weapons, ammunition, and explosives—more than enough to take out the bridge down the other side of the mountain and trap Steele's shipment of girls.

Trevor and Jax suited up in climbing gear, their harnesses full of C-4, and repelled down the bridge's stone support columns to place the charges.

Trevor swung out over the frozen river below, looking at the height of the massive old structure. "Do you think the state will send us a thank you letter? We're saving them a lot of work."

Jax smiled begrudgingly. "I don't expect they will."

Cowboy repelled down the stone column, pockets full of detonators. "So, about Olivia…"

"Forget it, Cowboy, she's spoken for," said Trevor.

"Shit." He inserted a detonator into a block of C-4 and wrapped the plastic explosive around it. "She looks a little like Brooke Barrons, you know? That woman is smoking hot."

Jax's head snapped up.

"She is Brooke Barrons," said Trevor.

Cowboy punched him in the shoulder. "No way, dude! You made it with a movie star?"

Jax held up his hand in Cowboy's face and turned to Hawk. "In all seriousness, she really is Brooke Barrons?"

Hawk shrugged his shoulders. "Yes, she really is. I told her that, but I'm not sure she actually remembers. Her memory's a little like Swiss cheese from the accident, but it's coming back a little at a time."

Jax's expression was deadly serious. "How do you know?"

Hawk grinned. "I had no idea you were a fan."

"I'm not," said Jax. "I repeat, how do you know

she's Brooke Barrons?"

Cowboy cocked his head. "What's going on?"

Hawk shrugged. "She's got a little tattoo on her ass that says Brooke. Why? What's the big deal? Y'all never met a famous person before?"

Jax turned back to Hawk. "Yesterday afternoon, Brooke Barron's big benefactor went on TV to ask for the public's help in locating her. He claims the two of them are engaged."

"It's all right. I already know she's engaged."

Jax continued as if he hadn't heard. "His name is Marco Acero."

"Should that ring a bell?" Hawk asked.

"*Oh, fuck,*" said Cowboy.

Jax narrowed his eyes at Hawk. "Do you know what Acero means?"

Hawk furrowed his brow. "Means?"

"I grew up by the Mexican border," said Cowboy. "And Acero is Spanish for Steele."

CHAPTER 31

THE OUTSIDE OF HERO Force Chopper One looked like something out of a military movie, but the inside was a surprise. Divided into two sections, the forward compartment had leather seating for eight, with what seemed like two computer monitors and a shiny metal console of some sort.

Olivia had gotten to see the rear compartment when the guys unloaded some unusual vehicles from the back, but it was the arsenal of weapons on the walls that really captured her attention.

The men had been gone more than an hour—possibly two—and she was grateful for the warmth inside the chopper and the relatively luxurious accommodations. She was also grateful for the time to be alone and think.

Now that HERO Force had arrived, her time in

the cabin with Trevor was at an end. She wasn't sure what that meant for them or, even more pressing, what it meant for her now that she had nowhere to go.

You must have a home somewhere. You just need to remember where and find it.

She scoffed. Easier said than done.

She truly hoped the relationship with Trevor would continue after the snow melted and the roadways cleared. She liked him far more than she should after just a few days, and in some ways she suspected she would always feel like he was her whole world—just as she had felt before her memory began to return.

He was that kind of man.

Standing up, she walked over to the console and began looking at the different controls, words popping out from the chaos of buttons and dials.

Infrared.

Radar.

Launch sequence.

Periscope.

I thought periscopes were only for boats.

She walked back and forth down the miniature aisle, her mind floating over the moments she'd spent with Trevor. His kindness. His strength. How well matched they were in the bedroom.

They probably didn't even live in the same town. That posed a problem. She wondered if her acting career was easily transferrable to another place, and if

Trevor would think she was stalking him if she followed him to the edge of the world and back.

She laughed at her own thoughts.

Stalker-ish, indeed.

The chopper door behind her rattled, and she grinned widely as she turned around, happy the men had returned so soon.

But the door was not opening, it was simply shaking, the handle jiggling as someone on the other side tried to get in. A metallic taste took hold in Olivia's mouth.

The taste of terror.

A man's voice called out, "Let me in, Brooke!"

Trevor called her Olivia. Anyone else from HERO Force should be able to get inside without her help. Still she yelled back, "Who are you?"

Trevor had told her the windows and doors were bullet-proof. As if on cue, someone fired into the window she was staring at. The damage looked like a bullet-sized chip in the glass, and she screamed as several more shots were added to the collection.

She dropped to the ground in a crouch. For a moment she considered trying to fly the chopper, then quickly dismissed the idea as idiotic. She needed to get to the weapons, but if the rear compartment was connected to this one, she had no idea how.

Gunfire continued as she crawled to the wall separating the two rooms. In the dim light from the single small fixture, she ran her hands along the baseboard, searching for some kind of opening mechanism. Finding none, she moved higher.

The gunshots stopped, and Olivia wondered if that was a good sign or a bad one. Several of her fingers scraped against something sharp, slicing her skin open and making her bleed.

There has to be a way into the other compartment from here!

A loud squeaking noise rumbled through the chopper. What was he doing out there? Another round of gunfire, though this time it sounded like it was coming from a different direction.

Her hand grazed over an electric control, and she quickly pressed it down. Relief was instantaneous when the door between the seating compartment and the weapons room began to slide to one side. As soon as she could fit her body through the opening, she threw herself into the darkness.

Straight into a man's thick, muscular arms.

"Thanks for opening the door, Brooke." He laughed.

The smell of body odor assaulted her nose as she swung her arms violently, hitting him in the face, but he only grabbed her wrists and cursed loudly in her ear.

"Stop it! I ain't gonna hurt you."

She continued to fight and he tightened his hold on her until it was nearly impossible for her to breathe.

"That was real funny what you did, Brooke. Setting me up with that chick and then running away. You're a goddamn comedian, you know that?"

"Let go of me!" she whimpered, working to get her knee between his legs so she could pop him in the groin.

"I don't know what the fuck's gotten into you, but we gotta go see Marco."

Olivia stopped moving. "Marco?"

"Yeah. He's been worried sick since your sister told him you didn't show up at the airport."

My sister. I have a sister!

The image of a twenty-year-old girl with curling black hair came into her mind.

"Bella?" she asked.

"Yeah. Now are you gonna stop trying to kick me in the nuts so we can get up there, or do I have to restrain you or something?"

"I want to stay here," she said.

"Well, that ain't an option."

"I'm not going back to Marco."

He smiled. "What, just because you're banging some guy in the woods, you think you and Acero can't live happily ever after no more? I won't say nothing if you don't."

She felt sick, the metallic taste back in her mouth. "How do you know about that?"

"I been looking for you, Brooke. And I found you,

too, back when I still had the snowmobile. You two've been doing without a fire for no good reason." He chuckled. "And let me tell you, you two are like a couple of really loud rabbits."

Embarrassment flooded her.

"Now come on, hot lips, it's time for us to go up the mountain. I took my snowmobile back after you left today, thank you very much."

"I'm not going anywhere with you."

"Oh, no? See, here's what I'm thinking. Marco wants me to find you, so if I find you, we're good. But if I can't find you, I'm still in deep shit, so I might bring him your new boyfriend instead."

Her eyes widened. "Trevor has nothing to do with this."

"You're fucking kidding, right?"

"What?"

"Jesus, you ain't kidding." He shook his head and laughed. "What are the odds of you dirty dancing with the exact same guy who's got a beef with Marco?"

Olivia went still, a horrible image beginning to emerge from the dots she'd yet to connect. She swallowed hard. "What do you mean, a beef with Marco?"

"They've got a history, those two."

"Marco and Trevor?"

His brows drew together. "I thought his name was Hawk."

She suddenly felt dizzy.

Trevor was after Marco.

Marco was the one who killed Trevor's friend, Ralph.

Trevor's words came back to her. *They're going to help me go after Ralph's killer.*

"Take me there," she said.

"I thought you didn't want to go."

"Damn it, whoever you are, just take me there! Now!"

CHAPTER 32

S HE LOOKED A little like Brooke, and that was his undoing.

Marco Steele always kept a firm hand on the reins of his emotions. He knew better than to mix business with pleasure, and he sure as hell knew better than to touch the merchandise. But she looked like Brooke, just a little around the eyes, and a hand reached out of the cavernous abyss of loss he'd been skirting since she disappeared.

Mister, you want blow job?

He closed his eyes as he let out a deep growl. She wasn't doing it right, wasn't as innocent or experienced or just plain perfect as his Brooke. He pushed the woman's forehead away and grabbed his dick in his hand, jiggling it. "Lick my balls," he commanded. "Suck 'em deep into your mouth."

Her eyes were not like Brooke's at all, now that he could see them up close. No one would ever be as pretty as Brooke, or as perfect. He'd been a fool to think this woman could change that, but now he needed to come.

He opened his eyes to watch her. He tugged himself, harder this time. He wanted to fuck her mouth, but she kept doing it wrong and he was getting angry, which made him want to hurt her.

Or maybe it was because she looked like Brooke that he longed to wail her with his open hand until she screamed.

How could she do this to him? Didn't she know he loved her more than anyone else ever could? He'd taken care of her. Given her everything she could ever ask for and more.

If it weren't for him, she'd be no one, nothing at all. Olivia Grayson was nobody, but Brooke Barrons was a star.

Teeth scraped his scrotum, making him stiffen and shout. "Careful!" Closing his eyes, it was Brooke's mouth he was sinking into, and she loved the flavor of him, the intimacy of this act, even though Brooke had never taken him in her mouth.

A guy can dream.

She wasn't Brooke anymore. She was nobody, there only for his pleasure. When he was satisfied, he let go of her hair and she fell to the floor like a rag doll.

"Get up," he said.

Her worried eyes got big and round. "You be nice to me now."

He laughed and grabbed her wrist, pulling her down until she was bent over his lap. "That's not how this works."

He hit her sharply, his eyes closing again. "Now tell me you're sorry for running away."

She was silent.

He hit her again.

"I sorry for running."

He began to relax. "Now tell me how much you love me."

CHAPTER 33

H ERO FORCE ARRIVED at Steele's compound in the last light of dusk, colors fading into grayscale, and stashed their vehicles in the woods nearby. Proceeding on foot, they made their way to the compound under the cover of pine trees that followed the perimeter.

Hawk's knee was much improved with the help of a splint from Logan, and he moved with speed and a practiced warrior's gait, his weapons harnessed and tucked all over his body.

The utility gate to Steele's compound was hidden around the back of the complex behind several dumpsters. Hawk only knew it was there because he'd been studying maps and satellite pictures. As the voice had promised on the other end of the walkie-talkie, the gate appeared to be locked but was, in fact, open.

The men filed in after him—Logan and Matteo on their way to infiltrate the communications and control systems, Cowboy on the grass just inside the fence to patrol for tangos, and Jax on Hawk's six as they went in search of Steele.

The compound consisted of four buildings: a large warehouse, Steele's private residence, a small office building, and a barracks for Steele's men. The residence was dark, so Hawk jogged toward the office building, moving nearly silently in his fatigues and combat boots.

Several windows were glowing, and he headed for the one farthest from the front of the building, hunkering down and peering inside. A kitchenette, empty. Next to it, a sitting room, also empty. The third window stopped Hawk in his tracks.

Steele leaned back on the edge of his desk, a naked woman kneeling in front of him. Steele threw his head back so that his eyes lined up with their hiding place outside the window, and Hawk and Jax both stepped back into the darkness.

"I don't think he saw us," said Jax.

"No, I think he's pretty busy." Hawk narrowed his eyes at the glass windowpane, focusing on the wire mesh inside it and tracing the wires back to a small box. "This window's wired to an alarm. If we take the shot from here, we get one chance and alert the tangos at the same time."

Jax shook his head. "I've got twenty bucks says it's bulletproof glass. We need to get inside. At least he's distracted."

The woman stood up and Steele turned her around.

"That girl's not more than twenty," said Hawk.

"I'm guessing she's closer to fifteen." Jax tapped his earpiece. "Logan, you in?"

A voice replied in their ears. "I've got the com system online. Working on the rest."

Hawk got a better look at the girl when Steele laid her across his lap and began to spank her. "She's not enjoying that," he said.

"Logan, I need you in that system!" snapped Jax.

"Two more minutes…" Logan sounded like he was physically exerting himself. "I'm in. I've got security cameras throughout the building and perimeter. Climate controls, electrical, everything."

"We've got a teenager being raped in the office building. Can you trigger the sprinkler system?"

"Give me a minute," said Logan.

Hawk and Jax made eye contact, knowing how much could happen in a minute. "If he doesn't get it in sixty seconds," said Hawk, "I'm firing into that room."

"He'll get it," said Jax.

They looked back through the window. The girl was sobbing openly now, and Hawk's finger twitched on his weapon.

The sprinklers went on in the room, water pouring out everywhere. Steele dumped the girl on the floor in his rush to stand, quickly running from the room as he held up his pants.

"Nice job, Doc," said Jax. "Now deactivate the alarm."

"Done."

Hawk moved to the kitchenette window. Steele was alone and appeared to be cursing as he dabbed at his wet clothes with a towel. Hawk moved on to the next room, which was dark, and turned on his night vision goggles. It was an office, a perfect point of entry. He took out glass and wire cutters from his pack and began to work.

He was nearly in when Logan spoke again.

"Uh oh, we've got trouble. Brooke Barrons just walked in the front door."

Hawk froze, his heart in his chest. "Olivia?"

"That's the one. She's with a man, considerably taller than her."

"Are you sure it's her?"

"My mom used to watch *The Young and the Restless*. It's definitely her," said Logan.

Hawk turned to Jax. "Why would she follow us? I told her to stay in the chopper."

Jax shrugged. "She's engaged to him. Maybe she wanted to be here. Logan, cut the sprinklers."

So Olivia had her memory back, and the first thing

she did was head out to see her fiancé. He wanted to bash his fist into something hard. She couldn't even wait until he came back to the helicopter to tell him where she was going.

"Wait a second," Hawk said. "How did she get here, Logan?"

"Let me rewind the surveillance video," said Logan.

Jax eyed Hawk intently. "It doesn't change anything, does it?"

"Hell yes, it does," said Hawk.

Logan's voice was calm in their ears. "Checking, hang on…"

Hawk's mind raced while he waited, looking for any other explanation for her presence here right now and finding none.

"Got it," said Logan. "She arrived on a snowmobile with the tall guy."

"Gallant," said Hawk. He met Jax's stare. "He's Steele's henchman. He's the one who tortured Ralph before Steele killed him."

"What the hell's he doing with her?" asked Jax.

Hawk shook his head. "I have no idea. But we can't assume she's here of her own free will." Even as he said it, he knew what the rest of the team was thinking. That he was a sucker, pure and simple.

He gritted his teeth and carefully removed the glass, placing it in the snow behind them. "On my six," he said to Jax, then entered the dark room feet first.

A phone rang in the distance as Jax climbed in behind him, and they slipped through the kitchenette and toward the open door to Steele's office.

"What is it?" said Steele into the phone. "It's about goddamn time. Do you know what it's cost me to feed these people for three weeks? What about the roads between here and the bridge?" He nodded. "Excellent. So we move them early in the morning. And tell D'jar there's a ten percent surcharge to cover unforeseen expenses. I'm not running a boardinghouse for third-world indigents."

Hawk strained his ears to hear the phone hanging up, then Steele talking again. Hawk moved closer, desperate for a visual.

"Yes, this is Marco Acero. Lieutenant Richards, please."

Hawk could just see the desk.

Steele hunched in his desk chair. It was several minutes before he spoke again. "Lieutenant, this is Marco Acero calling again. Is there any word on Miss Barrons?" He rubbed his temples. "I see. In the video, was she driving herself or was someone else driving?"

So he was trying to track Olivia down, and without much success. Trevor shifted silently onto his opposite arm. He couldn't get a good shot at Steele from this angle.

Logan was back on the com system. "Olivia and

Gallant are heading toward Steele's office."

Get off the damn phone, Steele!

Steele opened a drawer and withdrew a picture frame. While Trevor couldn't see what it held, he'd bet money it was a woman they both knew well, a woman who at that very moment was making her way toward this office and back into her fiancé's arms.

Bitter bile coated the back of Hawk's throat.

Steele continued. "I disagree, Lieutenant. She would not have left of her own accord. If she was driving, then clearly there was someone else in the vehicle controlling her actions." His hand balled up into a fist. "Fine, yes, I'll do that." He hung up the phone and leaned back in his chair.

Damn it.

He could only get a shot at Steele's arm.

A shot in the arm was better than no shot at all. He popped two bullets into Steele's left arm and sprung from his crouch on the floor. Jax was right behind him, weapon drawn.

Steele was screaming and pulled a gun from beneath his desk. Hawk shot it out of his hand before Steele could train it on them. Hawk knew he should kill him now, just like that, a few rounds to the chest and the bastard would be gone forever. But he wanted to see Steele suffer just like Ralph.

"Remember me, motherfucker?" he asked, his gun still pointed at Steele.

"Please…" Steele said, cradling one wounded arm with another and crying.

"It's important to me you remember," Hawk said, closing the distance between them. "You killed a good man the last time we met, and I want you to know why you're going to die."

The picture Steele had been looking at was now on his desk. It was indeed of Olivia, though in the photo she'd been much younger. A headshot from her early acting days, perhaps. Jealousy beat like a drum in his chest, anxious to control his body and tongue. "I know where your precious Olivia is."

Any color left in the other man's face drained at the mention of her name. "You couldn't possibly," he whispered.

"But I wouldn't really call her 'yours' anymore."

Steele's expression was pained. "If you hurt her, I will murder you!"

Hawk leveled his firearm at Steele's ear. "You're not going to get that chance. But I can assure you, I didn't hurt her. She loved every minute of fucking me." His finger moved to cinch the trigger.

"Trevor, no!" Olivia's scream wrenched from deep in her chest, and he turned around to find her and Gallant standing in the open doorway.

Gallant quickly wrapped his arm around Olivia's neck, holding her against his chest and a gun to her head. "You should listen to the lady," he said. "Because if you kill Marco, I'll have to kill her."

Gallant was a fool. He was so much taller than Olivia, she was no sort of shield. Hawk fired a round directly into Gallant's head, and the giant fell to the ground, pulling Olivia with him. She screamed hysterically as she freed herself.

"What are you doing?" she yelled.

"This is the man who killed Ralph," Hawk said. "He stood there and he watched as that useless piece of shit tortured him, then he took a knife and ended his life."

Her head fell forward and he thought she might pass out, but she raised it again a moment later. "So put him in prison." She walked toward Hawk with a wobbling gait. "But don't kill him. I'm begging you."

"Why?" Hawk asked. "Does he mean that much to you? You can't stand to see the man you love suffer?"

"No. I want answers. I need to know what happened to Ellie and Frank. I have to get my entire memory back so I can move on with my life. I may not be able to do that if he's dead."

"Go on," Trevor said, sneering.

"What do you mean?"

"Keep going. You didn't get to the part where you feel like you owe him something for taking care of you all those years."

"That's not fair. It's not that simple."

"Sure it is, Livy."

She sneered. "Don't call me that. Marco has his problems…"

"Marco Steele is a human trafficker who raped a teenager on this desk not one hour ago."

She physically shriveled.

Hawk was screaming now. "Now how about you tell me how the *fuck* you ended up engaged to that monster?"

She crossed her arms. "None of your business."

"He's not who you think he is, Olivia."

"No, you're the one who isn't who I thought he was! You made your work sound noble. Important. But you're shooting an old man in the arm and telling him you slept with me! How honorable is that?"

Trevor wished he'd never met her, wished her car hadn't gotten stuck in the snow, that there hadn't been any impediment between her and her lover on the top of this mountain of shit. "We're done here." He turned on his heel.

"It won't bring Ralph back, Trevor," she said.

He kept walking.

"If you care about me at all, let the police handle it. If what you're saying is true, he'll go to jail. You don't need to kill him."

He spun around. "Don't you understand? *I want to kill him.* I want him dead and I want to be the reason he stops breathing. I want revenge, damn it! I want him to pay for what he did."

"Then do it for me," she said. "Keep him alive for me."

"Because you love him?"

Jax fired his gun behind Hawk, and everyone turned to see what happened. There was Steele, blood spreading on his abdomen and a different gun dangling from his hand.

"The last shot is yours if you want it," said Jax, looking at Hawk.

Hawk looked to Olivia's eyes, then lifted his weapon and trained it on Steele.

"No!" Olivia's piercing scream echoed in the room, and Hawk's determination wavered. While there was no question in his mind Steele deserved to die, he suddenly wondered if Olivia deserved to watch her fiancé be shot to death.

Hawk lowered his gun and looked pointedly at Olivia. He would do what she asked. He would let Steele live, if only because she asked him to.

Jax moved closer to Steele and pulled out a pair of handcuffs, but they got stuck on his tactical suit and Jax bent his head to free them. In the split-second he was turned away, Steele shoved his good arm underneath his desk.

He's looking for a weapon.

No!

Hawk raised his gun once again, training it on Steele at the same moment Steele pointed a gun at Jax.

Hawk pulled the trigger, a perfect shot right into Steele's chest.

Jax's head snapped to Hawk's. "Holy shit," said Jax.

"How could you?" asked Olivia.

Hawk turned to see her standing right where she'd been, staring at Steele, and knew she was going into shock. Jax knew it, too, because he said, "Logan, send Red and Cowboy to free the prisoners. We need you down here for a medical eval on Olivia."

"I'm sorry," said Hawk, but she didn't seem to hear.

Hawk looked long and hard at Steele's dead body, then turned and walked toward the door. Olivia would never forgive him for this, but he couldn't forgive himself if he'd let Steele kill another one of his brothers.

CHAPTER 34

T HE HERO FORCE men made it back to the chopper and stowed their weapons and gear. Matteo settled into the pilot's seat while Cowboy, Logan, Hawk, Jax, and Olivia buckled into the passenger compartment for the ride.

She hadn't spoken to Hawk since he killed Steele.

"Where are we headed?" asked Hawk.

"We're working out of Gamma Squadron's facilities. We'll stay there tonight," said Jax. "Olivia, you'll spend the night in the infirmary."

She nodded.

"Someone should call Jessa when we get back," said Cowboy.

Hawk frowned at the mention of Ralph's widow, her name so deeply engrained with the painful memory of Ralph's death, though Hawk was grateful they finally had some good news to give her.

"I'm driving out there when we get back to Gamma Squadron," said Jax.

Hawk's eyebrows went up. "To Ralph's place?"

Cowboy looked from Hawk to Jax. "What is that, like, a fifteen-hour drive?"

"Sixteen," said Jax.

Hawk and Cowboy exchanged a look.

"Jax, have you kept in touch with Jessa since Ralph died?" asked Cowboy.

"No."

Matteo started the chopper, the noise instantly discouraging further conversation, even as the men donned communication headsets.

Jax looked out the window and Cowboy looked at Hawk, making a classic female hourglass shape with his hands, exaggerating the size of the ass, and pointing at Jax with a wink.

No way.

While it was true Jessa McConnell had a beautiful behind—one of Jax's favorite attributes in a woman—there was no way Jax was interested in Ralph's former wife.

Right? That would be too…weird.

Cowboy's voice came over the com set. "You know, Jax, I slept in the chopper on the way down. I can drive out to Jessa's place if you want. Give you a chance to sleep."

Hawk looked sideways at Jax to gauge his reaction. He'd swear the other man's posture stiffened at the suggestion.

"Nope, I've got this one, Cowboy," said Jax. "But thanks for the offer."

CHAPTER 35

NINETEEN HOURS LATER, Jax sat in his car and stared at the pale yellow house across the street. A tire swing hung from a tree in the yard, and he imagined Ralph's son or daughter playing there alone.

Had Jessa had a boy or a girl? Either way, it ate Jax up inside to think of the child growing up without the dad who would have loved him so much.

The child would be beautiful, he was sure. Even half of Jessa's genes would have made certain of that. He imagined she'd had a girl with black hair like her own, the Cherokee blood showing strong in the little girl's face.

And she'd never know her father.

It was Jax's fault. All of it. His decisions had gotten Ralph killed, and Jax ate, slept, and bathed with the weight of that responsibility every day.

He'd driven all night to get here, not stopping to sleep and barely allowing himself to think as the seasons flew by his window. He owed Jessa that much. Hell, he owed her a lot more than this, but that was a debt he'd always be unable to pay.

Fatigue pulled at him, weighing him down as he stepped out of his car and made his way up the walk, flanked by rows of pink and purple flowers on either side.

What had the last two years been like for her?

Grief could change people—make them bitter—but she'd have had to stay strong for the child. Surely the baby would have brought her joy despite everything she'd lost, tempering the blow.

Maybe she'd even remarried.

The thought put him off. His own mind had yet to move on from Ralph's death, and he couldn't believe she would have been able to, either, even though the men must be on her like bees on honey.

She was a spitfire—all long legs and loud laughter that made it clear Ralph was the light of her life. She just glowed, in a way he'd never seen a woman glow. She was…mesmerizing.

He rang the bell and waited, his palms damp.

The front door opened and she appeared, her dark hair hanging straight to her waist, just as he remembered.

His chest felt tight. "Hi, Jessa."

Something was different, an aloofness in her stare, and he was disappointed the light he remembered wasn't shining today.

"Jax." She crossed her arms and leaned on the doorjamb. "What are you doing here?"

The action pushed her breasts together and her cleavage poked out of her shirt. Tiny beads of sweat dotted her chest, along with a rosy flush, as if she'd been working hard.

"Can I come in?" he asked.

She hesitated before stepping back for him to enter. The living room was nearly empty, a few open boxes scattered about and the carpet rolled up, a broom leaning against a wall.

"Are you moving?" he asked.

"Yes."

He was aware of the tension in the air, the way she didn't invite him to sit down or ask how he'd been, but he longed to know how she'd managed with the baby and where they were going now.

He shoved his hands in his pockets.

"You look tired," she said.

"I drove all night."

"Why?"

Eight hundred days he'd been waiting to say the words, more than two years of wishing for this moment to arrive, imagining what it would be like to ease her pain the only way he could. "We got him, Jessa. Steele is dead."

The slightest lift of her chin was the only indication she'd heard him. She almost looked…

Angry.

He shook his head. "I'm sorry it took so long. I wanted to take him down earlier, I really did, but…"

"Get out."

"What?"

She raised her eyebrows. "Get out of my house."

"I don't understand. I thought you'd be happy."

She pointed to the door with her whole arm. "Take your sorry, cowardly ass, and get the fuck out of my house, now."

He'd never heard her swear, never seen her angry at anyone, and he wondered where the baby was that she would use language like that without concern.

She was always so gentle, so kind.

She hates me.

That much was clear.

He nodded. He walked to the door, then met her eyes one last time. "I'm sorry, Jessa. I really am. If you knew how often I think about you and the baby…"

She stood up and stormed to the door. "Just go!"

It was then that he really saw the pain, the tears waiting to burst from her eyes and the tightness she held in her shoulders. He stepped out into the sunny day, his eyes catching again on the pink and purple flowers that hinted at happiness inside, and turned back to her. "What happened?" he asked.

Her face crumpled and she slammed the door between them.

CHAPTER 36

JESSA STARED CRITICALLY at herself in the mirror and took a sip of wine.

Her silver tank came together just beneath her neck, leaving the tanned skin of her collarbones exposed on either side. She wore no bra for the straps to show, her pert breasts tenting the fabric of her shirt suggestively.

She turned to the side, a swath of golden skin showing between her top and her white jeans, the tiniest strip of hot pink panties visible at her waist.

Her makeup accentuated her best features. Gray eyes, full lips, shapely brows.

She was ready.

Unless time had changed the leader of HERO Force, Jax would be easier to find than a toucan on a sandy beach. Summerville had exactly one hotel, which just happened to be situated directly across the street from its only bar.

He was exhausted and it was over two hours to Dallas, so he'd be staying the night in town. But right about now, he would be at the bar drinking whiskey. If she was lucky, he'd been there for a while.

The slightest jangle of nerves rattled in her stomach as she pulled out of the drive, but she never wavered in her intention. Jax Andersson had taken away the only two things that mattered in her life—Ralph, and the baby she'd miscarried when Ralph died.

No one could bring her husband back, but in the hours since Jax left her house, she'd realized he could give her the only other thing she wanted.

Jax Andersson owed her a child, and it was time for him to pay the piper.

CHAPTER 37

JAX ANDERSSON PACED around the conference table. "You used HERO Force intelligence and weapons to fulfill a personal vendetta."

"Ralph had a right to justice," said Hawk.

"I have a right to know what the fuck is going on in my unit."

"You'd have told me not to go."

"Damn straight I'd have told you not to go. You'd be sitting in a federal prison right now if Steele hadn't been involved in human trafficking."

But he was, and Trevor and his fellow HERO Force members were being lauded as real heroes by every major media outlet in the land. Steele had more than a hundred people locked up in his compound. If that bridge hadn't blown, he wouldn't have gotten caught at all.

Jax braced himself on the table. "I've got to know that you're being honest with me. That this team is your first priority."

"It is now, Jax."

"How many of the team knew what you were doing?"

Trevor set his lips in a firm line. "I won't answer that."

"Son of a fucking pup." Jax ran his hand through his hair. "Tell me why I should keep you on HERO Force, why I shouldn't can your ass and find somebody else?"

Trevor stood and pushed his chair in. "Because I'm the one you want on your six. You know it and I know it. When it starts raining flaming shit, I'll get you out of there or die trying."

"Not good enough."

"Because I saved your life back at Steele's even though I knew it would cost me Olivia."

Jax stared at him for what seemed a long time. "Fine. We go wheels up in five days. Can you do that?"

"I can."

"Some Columbian drug cartel."

"I'll be there."

"And Hawk?"

"Yeah?"

"You didn't get the girl."

"Excuse me?"

"You gave up. You didn't die trying when the flaming shit started falling from the sky."

"That's different."

"I've got your six, too, Hawk. And you and that woman have unfinished business."

Hawk narrowed his eyes. "Speaking of unfinished business, how'd it go with Jessa?"

Jax turned his head slowly, leveling his icy gaze on Hawk. "Fine."

"Was she happy?" asked Hawk.

"No."

"Glad to see you?"

"You should go see Olivia before we leave town. Now get the fuck out of here."

CHAPTER 38

O LIVIA'S EARS WERE ringing through the valley of the shadow of death. The only things she could see were the petals of the flowers on Marco's casket trembling in the rain. Hard to believe he was in there, that the spirit had left his body, just like that.

Just like Ellie and Frank before him.

She suspected Marco had them killed, though she would never know for sure now. The Office of Homeland Security had filled her in on some of Marco's illegal activities. Combined with what she already knew, it was no longer a stretch to imagine he was capable of the things he was accused of.

Guilt had been her constant companion these last three days, even though it made no sense. It just was, and it likely always would be.

Would you feel so guilty if you hadn't been sleeping with the man who killed him?

As if reading her mind, Bella took her hand and whispered in her ear. "It wasn't your fault."

Olivia dropped her eyes to her sister's shoes, a pair of heels too sexy for anyone's funeral.

Typical.

Since reuniting with her sister, Olivia had regained her memories of Bella, and most of her life, for that matter. It seemed she had nothing else to hide from herself now that Marco was gone.

She let her sister's hand go and gazed beyond their little shelter to the cemetery beyond. A movement in the distance caught her eye. A lone mourner too athletically built to be a civilian, and a rush of sexual awareness zapped through her, quickly changing to anger. What was he doing here?

A flash of light far off to her left snagged her ire, and her head spun to see it. The paparazzi was out in full force, though the cemetery had cordoned them off in a small section about two hundred feet away. Now that her memory was back, she was Brooke Barrons once again, with all that entailed. And the only thing more exciting than her announcement of who her fiancé had been was the news that he was no longer alive.

Bella gently turned her, and Olivia realized the service was over. People were mouthing condolences Olivia didn't hear as she felt Trevor's presence burning a hole in the back of her head.

She needn't have worried. He didn't approach her until the last of the mourners and photographers were gone. She was upset, the days between Marco's murder and now doing nothing to ease her pain.

He wore a dark suit and tie, and he walked through the rain like he wasn't even getting wet. His eyes, when she could see them, were sobering and still. "I came to pay my respects," he said.

Bella looked from one to the other. "I'll wait for you in the car." She walked away.

Olivia glared at Trevor. "Do you think that's funny?"

"No. This can't be easy for you."

The sincerity in his eyes was her undoing. Tears came for the first time since Marco died.

Why now? Why in front of this man, the one who was responsible for Marco's death and her own transgressions? All of the true mourners had left her unaffected, but the one man who was glad Marco was gone had managed to touch her heart.

He opened his arms slightly. "Come here."

She shook her head, the tears coming harder because she wanted to go to him more than anything.

"I'm sorry, Olivia."

She wiped tears from her cheeks. "For what?"

"For having to kill him when you asked me not to. For hurting you. For caring about you and making love to you. I was selfish." He rattled the coins in his pocket. "I wanted you, I hated him, and everything else be damned. Hell, if it weren't for me, you might have gotten to Steele's house that day after all, and things would have turned out very differently."

"I wasn't going to Marco's."

"No?"

She shook her head. "I was going to the cabin." She exhaled hard and rubbed her temples. "I needed to get my memories before I left him for good, to remember who I was when I stood on my own two feet. Ironic, isn't it? That I went there searching for my past, and I arrived there without one?"

He smiled a sardonic grin. "What kind of memories?"

"Photographs of my family and Ellie and Frank that were up in the attic. And I needed to face that house. I hadn't been able to bring myself there since they died."

The sky became lighter, and Olivia realized the rain had stopped. She stared at the heavy clouds, haunted by the questions she would never get answered definitively.

"Do you think Marco killed Ellie and Frank?" she asked.

"Yes."

She nodded and bit her lip. "I think so, too. I didn't need him enough when they were alive." She could see it clearly now, how Marco had used her dependence on others to mold himself into the perfect man for her.

If only she'd been stronger. Able to stand on her own two feet.

"What made you decide to end your engagement?" asked Trevor.

"I overheard Gallant talking to Johnson about the shipment they just got in." She looked at Trevor, then dropped her eyes. "They said some disgusting things. Things about the girls and what they would do to them. It didn't make sense, so I asked Marco about it and he flipped out, grabbing me by the arm hard enough to leave bruises and saying it was none of my business."

"I remember seeing the bruises on your arm after the accident."

She bent down and retrieved her purse. "I should get going."

"Olivia, I want to see you again."

She stood and shook her head. "No. That's not a good idea."

"I think it is." He took a step toward her, closing the distance between them. "Hear me out. I've been obsessed. For the last two years, I spent every free moment thinking about avenging Ralph's death. I was so focused on what had been done to him, what had been done to me, that I stopped caring about anyone or anything else.

"Then I ran into your car, and everything changed. My weapons were gone. Satellite pictures and maps. And there you were, helpless.

"Don't you see?" he asked. "Caring for you forced me to loosen my grip on my plans for Steele. I couldn't do both. I hated it, at first. I resented you. And then I started to like it. I started to like you, even more than I hated him."

He took her hand in his. "You saved me, and I fell for you. I fell for you hard."

Olivia's eyes were wary. "But you still wanted revenge, and you made sure you got it."

"But it was no longer the only thing I wanted in my life. And when you begged me not to kill Steele, I heard you. I wasn't going to do it until he pulled his gun on Jax." He turned toward her. "Give me another chance, Livy. Give us another chance."

She shook her head. "I can't do that."

"Because you don't want to, or because you feel guilty?"

"Because I am guilty." She squeezed her eyes shut, then quickly opened them. "And while you may like me depending on you, I think it's high time I learn to take care of myself. If I'd done that years ago, I never would have ended up with Marco in the first place."

CHAPTER 39

B ELLA PASSED OLIVIA the ice cream and opened another box of pictures. "It isn't your fault."

Olivia frowned, the muscles at the corners of her mouth pulling down hard. "If you knew what I did, you wouldn't say that anymore."

"So tell me. Tell me all of it."

Olivia shook her head. "I can't do that."

"Why the hell not? You're spending an awful lot of energy mentally flogging yourself. The least you can do is share the whole story so I can flog you, too." She held up a picture. "Is this Aunt Holly or Uncle Mark?"

"I have no idea."

"Maybe you're afraid I won't think what you did was so bad," said Bella.

"What do you mean?"

"Well, if I think it's understandable and oh-so-very-human, while you think it's the worst thing a person can do, you probably don't want to hear that. You're not ready to forgive yourself."

Olivia let her spoon sink deep into the ice cream, pulling out chunks of chocolate and fudge. "I don't deserve to be forgiven."

"Would you be so upset with yourself if Marco hadn't died?"

"I don't know." She pushed the ice cream away. "Probably not."

Bella sighed. "Come on, pass that over here." She reached for the carton. "Who was the hot guy at the funeral?"

"Trevor Hawkins."

"Is he the one you were stranded with at the cabin?"

Olivia nodded.

"While you had amnesia."

She nodded again.

"It doesn't take a rocket scientist to figure out what happened, Livy."

Olivia rested her cheek against the cool wood of the table. "I knew I was engaged to someone else, and I slept with him anyway." An image of them making love filled her mind, and she shook her head to clear it. "He's the one who killed Marco."

Bella's eyes went wide. "No shit? He killed him for you?"

"No! I asked him not to, and he killed him anyway."

"Wait. Why would the guy you were banging kill the guy you were engaged to if it wasn't to get him out of the picture?"

"You make me sound so wonderful."

"I'm not judging, Livy, just explain."

Olivia sighed. "Because Marco killed Trevor's friend, and he was about to kill another one."

Bella pointed with her spoon. "I told you Marco was bad news. Sounds like this Trevor guy did the world a favor. Are you in love with him?"

"What? Of course not. I barely know the man."

"Livy and Trevor, sittin' in a tree, k-i-s-s-i-n-g!"

"Geez, Bella. Why do I even talk to you?"

Bella had her eyes closed and was making out with an invisible man, her arms wrapped around nothing.

Olivia slammed her hand on the table and yelled. "Bella, I need your help, and you're making fun of me!"

Bella stopped. "I tried giving you advice first. It was good advice, too."

"Oh, yeah? What was that?"

"To stop beating yourself up for sleeping with the hot soldier guy in the cabin, and maybe even realize you stumbled into one of the best things that could ever happen to you, instead of blaming him for your mistakes with Marco."

"My mistakes?"

"Yes. Your mistakes. You're not pissed because Trevor killed him. You're pissed because you were ever engaged to him, and you feel some bizarre sense of duty to the bastard that makes you hate yourself even more. Am I close?"

Olivia stood up, putting the top on the ice cream and dropping her spoon in the sink. "I don't want to talk anymore."

"I'll bet you don't. But unless you're planning to lose your mind again, I think you're pretty screwed. You're going to have to think about it sooner or later."

Olivia stood at the sink, one hand on either side as she stared beyond her reflection to the twinkling lights of Los Angeles.

"Listen, I've got to get going," said Bella. "But I was hoping you could help me out again."

Olivia closed her eyes. "How much do you need?"

"Well, Kenny moved out last week and we were a few months behind on the rent…"

"But I just gave you money last month! What did you do with it if you didn't pay your rent?"

Bella counted on her fingers. "There's groceries, and student loans, and I needed a few clothes, and Kenny's car broke down…"

"I gave you ten thousand dollars."

"The cost of living in L.A. is outrageous."

"So get a job."

Bella crossed her arms. "You know I've been looking. It's not like I can just go do a movie and make a bazillion dollars like some people."

Olivia sighed. "I'll give you fifteen hundred. That will cover this month's rent and some groceries." She pulled out her checkbook.

"Fifteen…there's no way I can get by on fifteen!"

"I don't think I've been doing you any favors by giving you money." She tore out the check and handed it to her sister. "Here's food and shelter. You have to work out the rest for yourself."

"Fuck you, Olivia."

Bella stormed out of the room, the sound of the front door slamming moments later. Olivia went to the table and picked up Bella's ice cream bowl, walked to the sink, held it up high, and let it fall.

It shattered into a hundred tiny pieces.

Feeling slightly better, she turned off the kitchen light and went upstairs to bed, eager to forget both Trevor and Bella, if only for a while.

CHAPTER 40

HAWK HAD SLEPT for sixteen hours straight after returning from the HERO Force mission to Cartagena, Columbia. It was the first good night's sleep he'd had since he'd slept next to Olivia in the cabin and the longest stretch he'd gone without thinking of her since.

But now he was awake, and damned if she wasn't right back in his mind as he made his way to the small grocery store two blocks from his apartment. He grabbed milk and a bag of coffee and headed for the express line.

There, right next to the bubble gum, was a picture of Olivia on a tabloid. It was like a sucker punch to the gut.

Better get used to it. You're going to be seeing pictures of her like that for the rest of your life.

His eyes went to the headline.

BROOKE BARRONS IN LOVE WITH NAVY SEAL WHO KILLED FIANCÉ.

"Holy shit," he mumbled under his breath, snatching up the paper, dropping the coffee, and turning to page three. There, right next to another picture of Olivia, was his service picture from the Navy, a photo of the cabin where they'd stayed, and a grainy picture of the two of them talking after the funeral.

He quickly scanned the article, his eyes catching on several sentences. "According to a source close to Ms. Barrons, she had amnesia for much of their time in the cabin together. It was then that the two of them became intimate. Our source says Brooke is 'head over heels in love with the guy, but can't forgive herself for cheating on Marco.'"

Trevor looked up from the paper. "Well, I'll be damned."

CHAPTER 41

O LIVIA PUT THE tabloid down and let loose with a
screaming string of curse words, ending with
Bella. "How could you do it, you rotten, traitorous
bitch?" she screamed to the empty room.

Money.

She'd do anything for money.

Olivia would have preferred her sister make up a
story about Olivia spending weeks in the woods with
Sasquatch than telling the truth about something so
entirely personal and painful, to boot.

She sank down on the sofa and pulled the paper
close to her face so she could better see the picture of
Trevor. It didn't do him justice, but it was still good to
see his face, and she ran her finger along his photo.

Her cell phone rang. It was her agent, Carol.

Ignore.

She reread the article several more times. What if Trevor saw this? She frowned. He didn't seem like the type to buy tabloids, but the headline alone would be enough if it caught his eye.

Her phone rang again. Unknown caller.

Ignore.

It immediately rang again. Her agent again.

Olivia huffed and answered the phone. "Hi, Carol."

"Darling, have you seen the tabloid headlines this morning?"

"Actually yes, I have."

"So, is it true?"

Olivia wobbled her head back and forth and closed her eyes. "Yes, it's true."

"Which part?"

"All of it."

"Well, my, my! Isn't that interesting."

"Listen, I just saw this, and I'm not really in the mood to discuss how we can spin it to my advantage right now, okay?"

"But that's why you have me, darling. Because I'm always ready to spin things to your advantage."

Olivia's phone beeped. "Got another call. Gotta run."

She intended to hang up the phone but accidentally answered the incoming call.

Fuck.

"Hello?" she said.

"Livy, is that you?"

Her stomach dropped down to her knees at the sound of Trevor's voice on the line. "Yes, it's me."

"It cost me three personal favors and a hundred bucks in cash to get your phone number."

She couldn't help but smile. "That's all?"

"I would've had to prostitute myself for your address."

She laughed, nervous energy rising to the surface.

"Where do you live?" he asked.

"Nowhere near you, why?"

"Seriously, give me your address. I'm in town."

Her eyes opened wide. "What?"

"I'm in town. New York gets the paper before you, remember? I hopped on a plane."

Olivia covered her mouth with her hand. Trevor was here. He'd come for her after reading that she loved him. Emotion swamped her like a tidal wave. She didn't think she'd have a second chance with this man, hadn't seen how it was possible.

She rattled off her address. "I'm still in my pajamas," she said. "My housekeeper brought the tabloid home for me."

"It says I'm forty-five minutes away from you."

"It's rush hour, Trevor. Multiply that by three." She was smiling so widely now her face was beginning to hurt.

"Taxi!" he called. "Are you still going to be home when I get there?"

"Mmm hmm."

"You still going to be in your pajamas?"

"If you want me to be."

"I'd rather you take them off completely." He gave her address to the cab driver.

She loved their banter and the sexy implications of his words. "I'll let you do that when you get here."

"You're getting me excited, and I'm sitting in a taxi cab with a driver named Rahul."

She laughed out loud. "You'd better go, then."

"I'll see you as soon as I can."

She showered, then washed and dried her hair, finally choosing a lacy negligee to wear for Trevor. Only once did her mind start to get the better of her, dampening her excitement with worry and regret, but she smacked it back down and refused to be unhappy.

Trevor is on his way here!

She damn near skipped through her apartment, shouting with glee.

When the doorbell rang two hours later, she ran to it and opened it wide. There he was, standing on her doorstep, a fresh tan on his skin and a hungry look in his eye that had her pulling him inside and throwing herself at him.

He picked her up as they kissed, and she held on to him by wrapping her legs around his waist.

"I missed you so damn much," he said between kisses. "I couldn't stop thinking about you."

"Me, either," she said.

"Which way's the bedroom?"

She pointed and he all but ran there, plopping her on the bed and following her down with his body.

She'd never felt so alive, so desirable, *so happy*. "I didn't think I'd get to feel you on top of me again, or inside of me."

He cursed under his breath and sat up just long enough to yank his shirt over his head. "You just talk about making love to me and you drive me crazy."

He loosened his belt and she unzipped his jeans, reaching inside and freeing his cock from his clothing. She helped him take off his jeans and raised her arms when he pulled the negligee over her head.

Then he was inside her, neither one of them having the patience for foreplay, and just as quickly she was riding the wave of an orgasm. He was really here, he was really making love to her in her bed, and the knowledge that he wanted her so much was enough to bring on her climax.

But Trevor wasn't through. He kept thrusting and retreating until he brought her to the edge once more before seeking his own release.

Olivia held on to his shoulders, loving the weight of him holding her down, and kissed his salty skin.

"Was it true, Livy?" he asked. "What the paper

said. Was it true?"

She laid her head back on the pillow and met his eyes. "Every word. I confided in my sister and she sold them the story."

"Ouch."

"Yeah."

"Every word, Livy? Are you really in love with me?"

The answer was clear, and she was suddenly grateful for her disloyal sister and the winding path that had brought her to this moment. She nodded. "I am."

He smiled, laugh lines appearing around his eyes. "I love you, too."

"It's also true that I have a hard time forgiving myself for what happened, Trevor."

He touched her face. "As long as you let me love you, we'll find our way out of that darkness together."

Olivia lifted her head off the pillow and brought her lips to his, tasting him and kissing him softly. "Thank you."

He rolled her over so she was straddling him. "Oh, sweetheart, that's just the beginning."

WHAT HAPPENED BETWEEN JAX AND JESSA?

SHELTERED BY THE SEAL: THE INHERITANCE
HERO FORCE BOOK 2

Jessa McConnell assumes the identity of a coworker to secure her future, but finds her life in danger when she inherits a book intended for the other woman.

The only person who can protect her now is HERO Force member Jax Andersson, a former Navy SEAL and the unwitting father of Jessa's unborn child.

* * *

Sign up to be notified of
Amy's new releases.

Sign up here:
http://eepurl.com/yVjV1
or text **BOOKS** to **66866**.

Made in the USA
Columbia, SC
16 October 2023

24514859R00143